THE CYCLE

of

HATRED

LINO AROP KUOL

Cover design, typesetting and layout: Africa World Books
Unit 3, 57 Frobisher St, Osborne Park, WA 6017
P.O. Box 1106 Osborne Park, WA 6916

PART ONE

SLAVES &
THEIR MASTERS

Chapter 1

Bakhita Nyanut sat upright on her bed and watched blood sputter on her thighs. She massaged them gingerly, trying her best not to touch the blood. She prodded with her index finger. No pain. Just numb. Everything below her waist was devoid of feeling. Above the waist, only the heart raced. *God, I'm dying!* Sweat dripped from her forehead onto an old grey blanket that was her bedcover. Nyanut panted, feeling like something had been riding her and knew she had actually been ridden by master Abdallah. That knowledge stung her more than her sore thighs. This was the fifth time, and she had begun to suspect that she was unconsciously learning a trade, an abominable and forbidden trade among the Dinka. She worked in master Abdallah's restaurant, but she knew what she was being paid in food for. Not the restaurant work.

The door slid open, and a robust man walked in wearing a white robe. It was master Abdallah. That is what Nyanut called him. She had never learnt his second name. The man walked to her and grabbed her chin, forcing her to look up at his face. A smile began to form on his lips. She knew that smile well. *He's going to do it again.*

"Abdallah" Someone called at the door. He started. Then released Nyanut and made his way to the door but before he opened the door, he turned to her,

"Clean that mess and come to the restaurant, little bitch," he said, and walked out, slamming the door behind him.

Nyanut climbed out of the bed and used the blanket to clean her thighs. She stumbled and fell and stumbled and fell again. Tears began to well in her eyes. *Stop it stupid.* She didn't want to cry. Crying was a luxury that only free kids would afford. She wasn't free. It was also a way of asking for your rights. Nyanut wasn't sure she had any rights here, in Aweil town, a place miles and miles away from her home, or what was left of it. She stood up and slipped on her rugged skirt and grey UNICEF T-shirt, dirty and torn from overuse. Her grandma had told her back in Makom that Sudan was dying. She hadn't understood then how a country died. Now she didn't understand still, but she'd began to suspect that the death of Sudan would involve the death of people.

"Nyanuuut!" Master Abdallah called from outside

"Coming sir."

She trotted to the door and opened it to find Master Abdallah staring at her menacingly. He looked around and made certain that nobody was watching, then grabbed one of her breasts and smiled wickedly, leading her away, towards the restaurant.

* * *

The market was full of people buying and selling. Bakhinta Nyanut could tell from what they wore that most of them were Arab. Long before she had seen an Arab, her father had told her they were bad people that should be shunned, but if you needed food, you might need to bare with them. Scattered about the market were Dinka and Luo people, running all sorts of errands. Some fetched water, and others baked bread. They did the things they would never do in their villages, smiling. This was women's work.

Nyanut entered the restaurant and commenced work. She picked up dirty utensils and scrubbed with a local sponge. She immersed herself into work, thinking about trivial things like how the glasses she washed were made from common sand.

She was awakened from her trance by two young men carrying trays full of bread and whistling a tune she recognized as Akut Kuei's 'Piny ci Deng Nok' The land that killed Deng. she knew the lyrics well, and doubted master Abdallah would be happy to hear such a song. One of the young men stopped whistling when he spotted her and nudged his friend. They didn't like her. They called her the Arab man's plaything, but they also feared her. They moved quietly and emptied the trays of the fresh bread into a container. Then stalked off to the corner of the room to rest, before going out to fetch bread. They began to talk in low tones. Nyanut pretended to be busy and paid full attention to what they were saying.

"Man, they came again last night," the one called Bol said.

"Did you tell them we are ready?" Garang asked.

"How could I? See, we've barely collected enough supplies. Besides, Awuluic is flooded. That means slow movement and it's too dangerous given the patrols. "

"I am getting tired, you know. How much longer can we do this womanly work?"

"Calm down. We've got to figure this thing out. If the rumours about the train coming from Khartoum are true, we will leave, supplies or no. That train brings death along with it."

"We'd better figure it out tonight and quickly." Garang said, looking visibly agitated.

"Not so quickly, let's give it time. Quick decisions are short sighted and danger- "

Master Abdallah entered and eyed the two boys resting in the corner. He picked up a log from a firewood pile heaped outside the restaurant.

"Are you resting?" he hit Bol with the log, splintering part of it, "How dare you rest?" he hit Garang with the remainder of the log as the two young men scrambled out, taking empty trays with them. Blood dripped from Bol's head. Garang was luckier as he only was hit on the back.

Nyanut watched them go, disturbed that she didn't know what these boys knew. She had recently started eavesdropping to their conversations but found them discussing meeting people who visited them. She itched to know these mysterious people. Her guess was that these people had something to do with the Anyanya. Master Abdallah had told her that the Anyanya were bad people, they brought hunger to Mading Aweil by looting civilian properties and burning their gardens. For now, she had to eat. She scrubbed the rest of the utensils clean and placed them on the rack to dry, humming Piny Ci Deng Nok under her breath. She remembered that the following day was Sunday. She wanted to go to church but that would depend on master Abdallah 's mood. She had to humour him and that was hard. It involved blood and numb thighs, though a little price to pay for the information she hoped to find at church.

St. Daniel Comboni Cathedral looked magnificent as Nyanut approached it. The eerie sweet sound of the choir reached her ears, and she rejoiced in it. These hymns often went to her soul. She couldn't describe what her soul was exactly, but at the sound of the choir, she often felt something moved in her, something that felt as if it were rejoicing. Nyanut hoped that was her soul because that would mean she was not really dying like she sometimes felt. She walked into the cathedral and sat in the front row among the early arrivals. An imposing statue of the virgin Mary watched her. Beside the statue stood a wooden sculpture of Jesus on the cross. Nyanut bowed her head and closed her eyes in prayer. The priest in her village had baptized her Bakhita after St. Bakhita of Omdurman. Bakhita was once a slave. Did the priest perhaps have a vision of what would become of Nyanut to name her? The choir sang on and a sweet solemn excitement grew. She shed tears. That was her way of appreciating art. The prayers began and Nyanut immersed herself completely into the mass, singing along with the choir and making appropriate responses.

After the prayers, Nyanut approached the Reverend father. A short old White man of the Comboni missionaries of Verona.

"Good afternoon, Father," Nyanut said behind the man of God who turned swiftly.

"Good afternoon, daughter." he replied, taking in everything and then waving for her to follow. When they reached the missionaries' quarters, he told her to wait. Nyanut waited knowing well that the man of God's mind was already aware of what she wanted, given the rags she wore. Of course, she needed food, but she had a more urgent need today. The man of God returned with a packet of biscuits and a T-shirt. This man had been around in Aweil for long, so long that nobody remembered his real name anymore, everybody called him Abuna Dengdit. Abuna Dengdit handed the the T-shirt and the packet of biscuits to Nyanut.

"Peace be with you" he said and turned to go back to the missionaries' quarters

"Abuna Dengdit, I want to know about the Anyanya."

The man of God glanced around to make sure nobody had heard the little girl speak. Having assured himself that nobody had, he visibly relaxed.

"Follow me," he said and led Nyanut to the common room of the missionaries' quarters. He pulled out two wooden armchairs and sat on one while Nyanut sat on the other facing him. Abuna Dengdit looked at the young girl deep in thought, then sighed.

"That was risky," he said eventually, "That could get someone killed here in Aweil. The Arabs would think I recruit on behalf of the Anyanya. Your Father joined?"

"No," Bakhita said. Abuna Dengdit looked her up and down as if measuring her then shook his head

"Too young to join," he muttered

"Father, what do the Anyanya do? Are they good people? "

"They fight, " Abuna Dengdit said, "So that you and I can live free in Aweil town and worship God without fear. People have days of being good, young one and their cause is just, and so they use a wide range of efforts to achieve the greater good even if it makes them look bad. "

"They caused this widespread hunger?" Nyanut asked. Before Abuna Dengdit could answer, two soldiers in uniforms, bearing the insignia of Sudan Armed Forces walked in. They looked hostile.

"Go well little one, "Abuna Dengdit said.

On her way out, Nyanut glanced back and saw the two soldiers put handcuffs on Abuna Dengdit's wrists. She turned quickly and walked away, back to master Abdallah's house. She had to earn her food.

Chapter 2

She walked home, feeling tired and afraid of what the next hour would bring. Bakhita Nyanut, only fourteen, had seen enough in life to call herself a woman. She was powerful in her newfound status. She knew she could control men and she did, though the men she controlled did not include master Abdallah. For to control a man, a woman must be able to deny him. With master Abdallah, she didn't have a choice, the man literally owned her

Nyanut watched master Abdallah's wife walk towards her. She loved to confront her, but not her husband. *Stupid woman.* Nyanut had often wondered why Hajjat Aisha had never confronted her husband about his infidelity. She had arrived at the conclusion that the older woman was simply stupid, or there was a conspiracy to mistreat her.

Nyanut averted her eyes and looked down, twisting her fingers on her lap as the older woman walked towards her. Hajjat Aisha thought of her as a young and broken child. She had to act the part. People didn't take well to being proven wrong and much less so when they are were in a position of power over you. The older woman shoved a jerrycan at her as soon as she reached where Nyanut sat outside the restaurant, covered in dust. The older woman didn't say a thing, but Nyanut knew what was expected of her. Still, she didn't forgive the woman for being so stupid. After all, what is womanly charm for?

She found herself deep in thought as she walked to the borehole and remembered her village of Makom. She had played happily under the moonlight with her friends, dancing to the beat of the drum. She had even started courting. Until it had happened. She didn't want to think about it. It always made her cry. The damage was already done.

Nyanut walked off the road and went and leaned against a nearby tree using her hands as cushion for her forehead against the tree. She left that position and faced upwards towards the sky, willing the tears in her eyes to go back. She walked on after recovering.

"Ma ooo!"

Screams of agony reached her ears from a heavily guarded enclosure by the roadside. Soldiers stood outside the entrance, guns at the ready as if expecting enemy combatants to materialize from thin air. It was Aweil military prison. Nyanut didn't know what went on inside, but whatever had made grown up men scream for their mothers, she didn't want to know.

She placed her jerrycan in the long line of jerrycans waiting to be filled and settled under a nearby tree and waited for her turn. In her village, the young men would have flocked to her, trying to court or tells jokes. Not here. She was beautiful then. Now she was too dirty, too filthy to be approached. She believed contrary to what people said, that a girl was just as beautiful as what she wears and how clean she is.

A man walked to the borehole with his Jerrycan. Something about how he walked alarmed Nyanut. She could read trouble all over the Arab man. The man walked straight to where a Dinka man with traditional marks on his forehead was filling his jerrycan. He kicked the man's jerrycan using his heavy army boots sending it skidding. The Dinka man looked up, shocked. Anger overwhelmed him and he forgot himself. He delivered a kick to the man's jerrycan and accompanied it with a slap on the man's face. Nyanut and other onlookers watched, aghast. *Decided too soon,* Nyanut thought.

Soldiers closed in and caught the man, beating him bloody with the butts of their guns. They kicked him too, wherever their boots found until he was unconscious. The trouble-causing man bellowed a challenge to the the onlookers,

"Any other Jenge slave wants a fight?"All the men kept quiet and left the Borehole one by one until only Nyanut and a few other girls remained. Satisfied, they dragged the unconscious man towards the military prison.

Nyanut watched, displaying no emotion. She had seen much of the same and it now looked like a normal occurrence. The vacuum left by the confrontation made it easy to fill her jerrycan quickly, but she lingered at the borehole. The prospect of returning home wasn't exciting. Master Abdallah waited for her.

Limping men, crawling men, and others, half naked wearing only shorts with enormous wounds on their backs, began to fill the borehole grounds. It was time for inmates of the military prison to take a bath. Nyanut lingered around. It was dangerous to interact with these men, but Nyanut's curiosity overcame her fear.

She sat on top of her Jerrycan and waited to see what happened to these men and why they were in. She walked innocently and sat a little distance away from one of them, pretending to be searching for something in the sand.

"What happened to your back uncle." she asked, still searching in the sand. The man extended to where she sat, moving as if stretching. When he was near enough, he said,

"Don't even ask little one. These wicked men iron us like clothes."

"Iron you?" Nyanut asked, taken aback. The man nodded. and turned his back to her so she could see. All over the man's back were pentagonal shapes. Some red and fresh with dried blood while others were rotten with yellow pus sipping from them. Nyanut could smell rotten flesh. She wrinkled her nose, barely stopping herself from puking.

The man turned, taking care that the soldiers did not spot him speaking to Nyanut.

"We don't need to commit a crime to get these. Being a Southerner is crime enough," the man said, "I was arrested for being a Sudan People's Liberation Army spy. The last time I came face to face with the SPLA, they took half my cows."

"What about him?" Nyanut asked pointing with her tongue at a one-legged man who used a pole for support.

"Same thing. They cut his leg so that he cannot carry messages to the SPLA again." The man shook his head.

"My grandmother used to tell me that Sudan is dying," Nyanut said absent-mindedy. The man smiled.

"You are witnessing its death presently," the man replied and walked away to join his mates.

Nyanut picked up her Jerrycan and lifted it to her head. She had mastered this technique, no matter how tiny she looked. She walked home, disturbed. What was SPLA exactly? Why hadn't she ever found a member of the SPLA. Were they the same as the Anyanya? Why were there so many contradictions about them. Too many questions. She needed answers but she wasn't sure from where she was going to get them.

***

Bol Deng moved through the overcrowded Aweil market. Glancing left then right, then left again, he passed at the Domino club. No sign of Garang. He went to the bakery, still no sign of Garang. *What has the stupid boy gotten himself into?* Bol went back to the restaurant and sat down. Perhaps Garang would show up, after all he is a grown up. Bol expected that to calm him, but it did not. Something felt wrong. He wouldn't explain what, but it was there, that feeling that something was about to happen.

He kept looking up every time a customer entered, expecting to see Garang and was disappointed every time he saw someone else. Bol wouldn't even talk. Only the little girl was present apart from the customers, and he hated her, hated how she let that man use her. For Christ's sake couldn't the damned girl put up some resistance at least.

He waited agitated, awakened from his thoughts by the sound of gunshots from the other end of the market. Two gunshots so far, that's two bullets spent. He made a mental note of that and waited for more. None were shot again. SPLA haven't arrived then. It was too good for him to hope, he knew that.

Bol felt strange, like he was falling sick. The last time he had experienced this was the day he had lost his elder brother. *No!* He ran in the direction of the gunshots. He ran, caring for nothing. When he reached the scene, soldiers were pulling a corpse, dragging it onto a truck to dump in the swamps of Awuluic. Bol stood amongst the watching crowd. He recognized the clothes.

He turned and walked away, feeling empty. *It's My fault, why did I insist on staying here? Why!*

He staggered, then steadied himself and entered an empty stall. He cried beating his head on a table. He had lost yet again.

***

Nyanut watched the crowd, shocked. The soldiers were dragging Garang's corpse into a truck, holding him like a dead dog. The one who threw him on the truck was a Southerner. Nyanut hated the man for turning on his people. Somewhere in the middle of the crowd, she spotted Bol. He looked like he was about to run onto the scene and confront the soldiers. She found herself praying that he does not attempt it and get himself killed too. Blessedly, Bol turned and walked away, out of the crowd. They may not have liked her but still, they were closer to her than anyone else in Aweil town.

She wept silently in her heart. Two years back, she could never have watched such a scene, but a lot happened since then. Now, everything looked like an action movie and though it did pain her, she felt the pain far away, as if it was happening to someone else.

She walked out of the crowd, thinking and talking to herself. That was the only thing she had left. Thinking. She thought about everything and nothing. How was she going to find out about the SPLA? Abuna Dengdit had disappeared after she last saw him being kicked by two soldiers. Garang was dead, and next to die would be Bol. People always died on her. Her parents, her siblings. Everybody. Tears flowed freely from her eyes. She didn't even bother to wipe them off.

She found Bol carrying a sack out of the corner of the restaurant that had been his and Garang's sleeping quarters. He looked at her. Hostility written all over him.

"Sorry," she murmured and looked down.

"I'm leaving. Tell your master that he can shove his money up his ass."

"You really think I like him? "

Bol shrugged, "You do everything he tells you with no complaints. "

"Don't you think that means I'm afraid of him instead? "

"Whatever," Bol said, "I'm going to look for guns wherever I can find them. Garang will be avenged."

He threw the sack containing his meagre belongings on his back and walked away, disappearing into the thick market day crowds.

Chapter 3

Alor Biong saw it coming but he would do nothing about it. The slap landed on parts of his right ear and cheek, sending vibrations and disturbing sounds to his head. *Ignore it.* He continued writing, his book rested on his lap as if nothing had happened. The aggressor, a young boy wearing a robe and cap wasn't done yet. He came again, this time aiming for the book. He gave it a kick, sending the book and pen scattering in different directions. Alor's temper flared, like hot fire. He could feel it in his heart and his head. Raging. He aimed a kick of his own. It landed in the stomach. The boy granted. After a time, he rolled in the sand, his white robe turning brown.

"Right," The boy said, smiling and ran off.

God, what have I done. He knew he should never have kicked the boy. His father had advised him not to respond to their provocations. His mother had said the same. But Alor was finding it harder to restrain himself each time.

The boy returned, bringing along with him a bearded man. The man held a stick, though Alor thought it was more of a club than a stick. The young boy pointed at Alor and the bearded man took hold of him by the collar and started to be beat him. He screamed himself hoarse. Blood gushed from his mouth where the teacher had punched him. The man kept kicking and punching him, all the while shouting, "Will you beat him again, you are a brute, you little Jenge devil. "

When the man left him alone, Alor continued to cry but kept quiet after a while. This was not new. They always beat him. It didn't matter whether he erred or not. His young classmates just had to tell their teacher what he had done. That was, whatever they could make up. They reported him once a day. Twice if they felt especially wicked.

Alor didn't understand why his father kept bringing him back to the government school because he wanted Comboni. At least in Comboni, this kind of punishment was not allowed, did not exist as a matter of fact. The majority of the students there were Southerners or considered themselves Southerners due to the complicated situation of Abyei. The Arabs thought of Abyei people as Southerners but thought of the area as Northern.

The bell rang for break and Alor walked back home. His school session was over for the day as far as he was concerned. It felt like he was learning how to bear beatings. He wondered what such learning would make him. A camel perhaps.

Alor's father worked in the Sudan police service. That alone should have made teachers treat him better at school, but it was more complicated than that. His two older brothers had left home one night and never came back. It was assumed they had gone to join the SPLA. That put his family into the regime's bad books.

***

A land cruiser pick-up full of soldiers, muddy from passing along feeder roads, pulled up in Alor's neighbourhood. It had rained heavily the previous days and water collected in pools everywhere in this neighbourhood. Green grass sprouted here and there, and frogs made age old music. They croaked with joy.

One soldier held a megaphone and stood up.

"All civilians this side of the Nyamora are hereby ordered to report tomorrow to the side of the Nyamora next to Colonel Yasin Mohammed 's residence with mosquito nets. You shall be expected to fish out noisy frogs that have been giving the colonel sleepless nights. Failure to do so... "

The announcer did not finish. He left it hanging and the civilians did not miss his implication. These men held all the cards. A person could disappear forever, and his family would have nobody to petition.

So, nobody said a thing to object. This was insufferable, but the people of Abyei had good reason to fear. These men had the entire arsenal of the country at their back. The elders had complained about the treatment once and only received a short note to their complaints. This note appeared nailed on trees throughout Abyei town one morning. It called upon the four complainants to show up in front of a firing squad next day, on the shores off the Nyamora, or risk their whole households being annihilated. The people did not doubt that these people meant every word of their threats. The four men had dressed up in their best attire and walked to their deaths, believing that by doing so they had saved their families. Alor wasn't so optimistic about that. Life and death under these people had a sinister resemblance.

* * *

The rains were falling heavily, for abnormally long hours this year. It was not good for crops, but it was good for the trees. They stood tall and green, swaying majestically in the wind. The rains were also good for the Nyamora. It was as full as it had ever been in Alor's living memory. Its surface shone like glass in the early morning sun. The tiniest of winds sent ripples across the surface. *Beautiful.* Alor liked it that way. He wanted to swim but nobody was allowed to. The people of his neighbourhood had come to fish frogs.

The most humiliating exercise that Alor had ever seen commenced. All the young men from the area lined the Nyamora in pairs, holding a mosquito net between them, having stepped one end of it down. They slid into the Nyamora like a group of dancers performing to perfection. Alor knew all the young men. He saw the humiliation in their eyes, and Alor felt it bit his heart like some stinging insect. His father's position in the police had at least saved him from doing this humiliating work. In theory. The reality was that Alor felt humiliated because what humiliated the Ngok as a whole, humiliated him too.

"You, what have you caught?" One officer asked a young man. The young man, too annoyed to speak, but too careful to risk a confrontation, opened his hand revealing two tiny tadpoles.

"Damn! You Jenge think you are clever," the man said, slapping the small tadpoles back to water, "Go back and catch a frog. A real fat one or tell John Garang to come and liberate Abyei." He kicked the young man, sending him staggering back into the water. Many got similar kicks and were told to go back and catch frogs.

Shit! Alor swore under his breath as he watched the exercise. How were people expected to fish out frogs in a water body as vast as the Nyamora? Alor suspected this had to do with power, people around him loved exercising it. To the extreme.

* * *

Mulmul residential area looked like a lit stage in the evening. Twinkling lights covered the compounds of all households, as women set to work preparing supper. Alor made his way to their homestead, all alone. He seemed to always be alone these days. Based on age and the common rules of nature, he shouldn't be thinking so much about the plight of his people. He should be laughing, chasing the occasional girl and sucking up to the Arab regime. But if he did that, he wouldn't be Alor anymore.

"….and so, they dropped him into a boiling barrel of oil. Never did he flinch. He died with dignity and with a new message to the Ngok people not to surrender." His mother was telling a story to his younger siblings. Alor knew this story very well. His mother had repeated it to him so many times over the years that he had become too familiar with it. Alor had begun to question whether giving oneself up to be killed like the man had, was the right way towards Ngok liberation. This battle needed shrewdness not hot tempers.

Alor pulled a chair and sat down, completing the circle around the dining table. The other members in the circle in the middle of the compound included his father and uncles. They conversed in low tones, and Alor knew what that meant. Something was afoot. Sudan Police Service may have boasted of having Biong Deng as a first Lieutenant among its ranks, but the man was still a Ngok first at heart. Alor could smell the makings of a plan in the air.

His uncles' wives arrived one after another, bringing food to the mess. The conspiracy tone was abandoned, and jokes were picked up and laughed heartily to.

At long last, Alor's father clapped him on the back,

"Your uncle, Kuol has a proposal," he said, "he wants to take you along with him when he leaves."

"I'm in school, "Alor said

"I was of the opinion that you didn't like that school. Besides, your talents will be best put to use in a project your uncle is thinking of enrolling you into. "

"Am I going to Khartoum then? "Alor asked, childish excitement taking over him.

"No," his father said, "You are going to Kirrkou"

CHAPTER 4

❧

Two Years Ago

What became known as the scorching of Makom, so far as Nyanut could remember, began with the arrival of a man named Diing Wol from Kiir Adem. Nyanut had seen him arrive and he had been hard to miss because practically the whole village trailed the man until he reached his house. Around him danced a large swarm of flies. His clothes were red with blood, and he carried a bloody package tied to a small rope that hung from his neck like a necklace. His movement was impaired, and he moved sluggishly, dragging his feet and grimacing at every step. When people ran in to support him, he waved them away. He said he was strong enough to complete the journey he had started from Kiir Adem.

Nyanut knew the man well, he was her father's close friend and neighbor, but he had been two years in land controlled by the Arab regime, only to return now in such a state. As soon as Diing Wol stepped in his compound, his wife shrieked at the sight of him.

He staggered and almost fell and called for a stool. Blood gushed onto the stool when he sat, and Diing Wol screamed. He untied his gruesome package; something fell out of it and Nyanut heard everyone around her gasp. Someone said something about children being around, and Nyanut was barred from seeing what happened. The man died shortly after, and the village wailed. Mourning Diing Wol, once the village's strong man.

Nyanut neither heard nor saw anything throughout the commotion that day but being the curious child, she gathered bits of the story from here and there until she finally had the full story.

Diing Wol had gone to Meirem to work and having done his time there decided to return home to his family through Kiir Adem, but a Reizigat farmer there had offered him work on his farm and the pay was too good to reject. He had settled there and began his work but when the first month was done, his employer did not pay him. The employer had instead called Diing and commenced calculations. This, he would say, is your expenses for food, and that is your expenses for soap, so that at the end of the calculations, Diing owed the employer some money. The following month, Diing cut his expenses, but the debts mounted. The man would not let him go without paying. The money he had made in Meirem had run out. In short, he was now the Reizigat master's slave and the man had him watched, so escape was out of question. Diing then spent the two years working for food until one day, his master had come with two other men and assaulted him, wrestled him down and dismembered his genitals and tied them in a bundle which they made him wear like a necklace and told him to go back home.

The elders in the village spent the next few days deliberating their course of action, under the meeting tree near the Makom market. Nyanut sneaked in to listen. Her mum said that curiosity would be the death of her, but the little girl did not care. The discussions which had begun with the village united became divisive, the young men pitted against their older counterparts.

"Makomda, I greet you," chief Deng Achien saluted and cleared his voice, "It is unfortunate that such an event has occurred in our lifetime and among us. Never at any time in history have we experienced such a gesture of hostility from any of our neighbours. This is insufferable and must be responded to." he paused, and the gathering cheered, mostly the young. The old timers watched, grim faced.

"However," chief Deng continued, "It's not possible to respond in equal measure to these people. If we did so, and they accepted battle, we shall be pitted against an enemy with superior weaponry compared to our own." The old men nodded but the young people murmured something about cowardice.

"Shame on us. Our brother gets butchered and all we can do is talk of superior weaponry," A young man spat and Nyanut realized, with a chill, it was her elder brother Yel.

"Was it not with a spear that my grandfather Thou Dau chased two men and captured their guns? The weapons do not fight. People do." another young man said.

The deliberations went on for many days until at long last, it was agreed that tit for tat was a fair game. They chose a local Reizigat businessman to carry the sins of his kin. He was mutilated in like manner with Diing and sent crying and bleeding northwards. The elders hoped he died before reaching Kiir Adem, but the young men prayed he reached Kiir Adem so that his kin could feel the pain.

For months nothing was heard from the Reizigat, and it was assumed that the man had died en route to Kiir Adem, and the matter was forgotten. Until a cry went up in Makom one evening,

"The Arabs have come. The Arabs have come."

The village was practically surrounded at this point. Arabs emerged on horseback from the thicket surrounding the village and the onslaught began. The Kalashnikov rifles spat fire and people and animals fell. The assailants set granaries and huts afire and the whole village was a mess. Nyanut watched, she wanted to scream but could not. Wanted to run but could not. It all resembled a dream, and she had had many of these kinds of dreams. She knew the screaming would come when the dream was almost over.

"Nyanut, under the hut," someone shouted. She looked around but saw no one.

"Nyanut, under the hut!" the voice screamed at her again. She recognized it, her brother Yel, and she understood. She ran into the hut. More screams. The hut caught fire as she ducked in. She entered the tunnel at the back of the hut and began to crawl. Screams grew fainter as she crawled away. She kept crawling. When she reached the exit, she was too tired to move. She rested her head on her arms and slept.

When she woke, up it was morning and Nyanut found herself in the forest. Birds twittered gleefully in the trees. She knew this part of the forest well. She looked around. A few kids moved with bewildered eyes in the forest. All the escape tunnels in the village led this way. The events of the previous evening came rushing back to her. Hot tears rolled down her cheeks.

Slowly, older people came one by one for the kids. Nyanut did not see anyone from her family. The news was that the Arabs had left Makom. The little group began to move towards the village slowly as if each of them thought that if they took their time, Makom would go back to how it was before the attack.

Everything looked out of place in the aftermath of the Arab invasion. Circular walls which had been huts stood bare, throughout the village. Their roofs having been burnt. The pungent smell of burning sorghum greeted the few survivors but that was nothing compared to the general smell of the village as the dead lay covered in their own gore. The gardens were green, but the sorghum was trampled by horse hoofs and starting to wither.

Nyanut went to her home. or what had been her home. It smelled of death like every other household in Makom. Her mother lay near what had been the kitchen, saucepan still on the hearth stones. Her father and two brothers were nowhere to be seen, but there was no question of where they were. They were waiting to be buried in the large heap of the dead. Their cows had been taken as war booty. Makom was dead.

Chapter 5

Nyanut stood behind master Abdallah at the train station in Sika Adid wearing a grey tattered skirt with the sky-blue UNICEF T-shirt that Abuna Dengdit had given her, and waited for what her master said was bringing goods from Khartoum. Master Abdallah called it 'gathar'. He said that the primitive Jenge language did not have names for relatively new technologies like gathar. So Nyanut stood and waited for this unknown object that ran along a tiny metallic path.

The cling of metal and the hissing of the steamer reached her ears. She watched the long twisting railway line but saw nothing. The cling of metal increased. Then men emerged, some on horsebacks and others in small land cruisers. The mobile force. They spread in an orderly manner and Nyanut could see that these were well trained soldiers even though they wore no uniform and looked more hostile than any Arab she had yet seen in Aweil town. More emerged as the train finally came into sight. Nyanut had never seen anything like it. *No wonder my language has no name for it.* She watched it in awe and wondered how a thing as big as that could slide on two little metal tracks so accurately and not fall off. When its head reached the station, the train stopped. It hissed like quenched fire and gave up enormous smoke.

The carriages opened and men clambered on board to unload the goods meant for Aweil. Hostile men disembarked from inside some of them. Some of the men looked like Sheikhs, dressed in robes with turbans on their heads and with deliberately kept beards. They looked scary, carrying Kalashnikov rifles slung to their shoulders. One of them passed where Nyanut stood with master Abdallah and said something in his thick Arabic accent, pointing at Nyanut. She didn't get what the strange man said but master Abdallah replied with a smile in the same thick accent and his answer seemed to calm the man. Nyanut shuddered because she knew from experience that master Abdalah's smiles didn't hold anything good for her.

She picked up some of the things that had arrived from Khartoum while master Abdallah hired some men to assist her to carry the bulky stuff back home. Master Abdallah himself followed leisurely, making sure the men didn't stray with his goods.

As they walked home, Nyanut wondered who those hostile men just arrived were. Something was terribly wrong with them. From the way they talked to their overgrown beards and Kalashnikov rifles on their shoulders. More disturbing was the fact that they wore no military uniform and yet acted in every way like soldiers.

She let it pass. A lot of things did not make sense to her anymore, her body included. Everything felt foreign. Blood flowed but no pain. Thighs numb but no aches. She walked on, trying not to think about the men but about the wonder she had witnessed for the first time ever, gathar. Try as she might, the question still came back stronger. Who were these men? Bol and Garang had once talked about a train that was bringing death. *Is this the one?*

There was one way to find out. She had to go out tonight. After Bol had left Aweil town, angry at the murder of Grarang, Nyanut lost her last link to the outside world. Necessity however forced her to find a new way of getting the information she needed.

She was going to do that today. She deliberately let master Abdallah have her early. She had noticed that he loved it when she cried. She did so easily, she faked tears, enough to wet part of her bed cover. It was easy. Sometimes she found it hard to believe she was only fourteen, she felt much, much older.

Master Abdallah at last sighed and fell back on the bed. Nyanut quickly cleaned herself and slipped out of the room and onto the streets of the market. She turned a corner and moved swiftly. Her destination was an area lined with bars. The bars were dimly lit with oil lamps, but something felt wrong. The bars were unusually quiet and quiet places in Aweil meant danger. She walked cautiously and listened; someone was sobbing in the nearest bar. A woman. Not good. Siko and other alcohol smelled strongly in the air. She froze. Someone was pouring the drinks nearby. The drinks splashed to the ground like water.

"You intoxicate and seduce men with your drinks. Sending them to eternal damnation." someone was saying in a hostile voice, in a thick Arabic accent." This was followed by sobs from a woman.

"You abandon all other economic activities to sell a sinful drink!" more lashings and sobs.

Nyanut tip toed to an opening at the back of the bar's grass fence. An Arab man stood over a southern woman with a horse whip. One glance told her she needed to get as far as possible from the bar.

* * *

Master Abdallah sat under a palm tree in his compound and

listened to President Nimeiri's declaration of sharia for the Sudan. He had recorded it and always listened to it as. He listened attentively, as if this was new to him, as if the president were speaking at that moment. He could relive these moments in his head, because he had been there when it all happened.

He had seen President Nimeiri back up his declaration with action, though he thought the President rather did it with excess zeal, bulldozing two million dollars worth of Alcohol. Master Abdallah had almost screamed, "Export that shit you dummy." Then he had only been an onlooker and had he dared, he might have been crashed by zealous Islamists. Master Abdallah himself had nothing against Islam but he believed Islam was best when used to oppress the Southerners. He wasn't sorry for the man when he was toppled. He had not done what he hoped he would after sharia. He turned out not to be the chosen one. Not even close.

The first part of the record finished playing and Master Abdallah increased the volume. Marshal music began to play, marking a new chapter in Sudanese politics. He had arranged all to reflect the Sudanese political landscape. That way, the record kept its original aspects of surprise and felt too good to be true. A new declaration then played. Dr. Hassan Al Turabi spoke, and Master Abdallah listened, tears welling in his eyes. Dr Turabi always made him nervous when he spoke. The man was learned, and it showed in his speech. Turabi was now declaring Jihad on the South, a holy war. Almost too good to be true. Master Abdallah hadn't listened to this record in a long time.

He now listened and as he did so, imagined the mujahideen engulfing the South, consuming the infidels like the locusts consume the greenery. He had imagined this for years, the fall of the infidels. One thing had been missing in his imagination, his mujahideen had been faceless. That had changed today, now he knew what they looked like. He had seen them alight the train at Sika Adid the previous day and they were more than he had dared hope. They looked and smelled like terror. The perfect package.

CHAPTER 6

Nyanut woke up with a start. She panicked. She had overslept and Master Abdallah would be waiting for her at the restaurant, but he might burst into the room at any moment. She opened the door, just a crack and peeped out and gave a sigh of relief.

Master Abdallah sat outside under the palm tree listening to the radio. A holiday of some sort perhaps. Eid al Adua, Eid al fitr? Nyanut didn't know which. Muslim holidays always confused her.

She went out. If it was indeed a holiday today, it was a free day for her. Not that she wouldn't be treated like a slave, she was a slave everyday, but her duties would be lighter every Muslim holiday. Other duties, that is. The rape was a steady thing. It came once every day, twice if hajjat Aisha was sick.

She walked about the compound slowly, wearing her best 'half-witted girl' look. The Arabs loved her that way. Cleverness was frowned upon, punished even. The Jenge was supposed to lack wits and if she had wits, they had better be half and the learning of that half better be attributed to interaction with the Arabs. Nyanut hated them, and this hate needed an outlet. She scratched her head. She wanted to join the SPLA more than ever now. *Do they recruit women though?* She wondered.

She passed by Master Abdallah who never looked up. He was too absorbed, listening to the radio. She stopped abruptly. What was that? Master Abdallah was crying. Tears rolled down his cheeks. Unless those were tears of joy, she did not believe such a monster was capable of crying.

She hurried away towards the market. Maybe her run on the previous night had been exaggerated, maybe the bars were alright. She reached the bars section of the market. It was all ashes. Nyanut didn't doubt that some of the owners had been burnt too and the ordeal of the previous night was real. *What is wrong with me?* She had begun to view most events in her life like dreams. She wondered whether perhaps as life became harder, her brain was trying to delay imminent madness by presenting everything like a dream.

Someone brushed against her while she stood watching the ashes that had been the bars. Just a slight touch.

"Follow me," the person whispered and walked away, as if nothing had happened. The voice was familiar, but she couldn't place a name to it. Nyanut found herself torn between two impulses. Her first impulse was to turn and run in the opposite direction, to safety. The second impulse was of curiosity. Such things didn't happen often. She wanted to find out what the man had to say because he looked Southern, the part of his face that was visible at least.

The man's face was covered with a green scarf. He was a young man from Nyanut's estimates, twenty at most. She trotted behind him. Keeping a little distance while the man walked on as if he had said nothing. Maybe she had only imagined it. Nyanut fought the urge to turn and walk back. She barely kept up with him. It took a lot of effort given her frail malnourished body.

"Hayya alas-Salah!"

Somewhere in the town mosque, the muezzin called the faithful to the afternoon prayers. The man in green scarf kept walking, turning corner after corner and Nyanut kept up. She had seen enough suffering to fear a single man.

They turned yet another corner and the man turned abruptly yanking off the the scarf. Nyanut blinked

"Bol?" Nyanut said.

"The very same" the man said "I remembered that you had no other choice than following your master's orders. I've come back with a new choice" Nyanut smiled

"Let me guess, the new choice is escape."

"Would you rather serve him?"

"No. But how do we survive on the road to wherever we are going when I hear that there's no food in the countryside."

"That's a good question. The answer is that our escape is an organized one. We have accumulated some supplies."

"We?"

"Of course, there's about two dozen of us."

Nyanut thought about it for a moment.

"Let's get going," she said. Bol cocked his head

"Just like that. No luggage?" Nyanut just eyed him

"I'm my luggage," she said, and Bol laughed.

Bol wrapped back the green scarf over his head so that it covered much of his face and walked ahead. Nyanut followed at a distance, moving swiftly through the market. Just another young Southern girl whose master had sent on an errand.

Ahead, Bol moved steadily, never looking back. She didn't know the road specifically but knew where it led. Alok, a town much smaller than Aweil. People said that this road they walked on led to Alok. Nevermind that many had never travelled there, but it was an unofficial Jieng custom, and people believe without caring much for factual verification. The theory of Kor Agaar, Nyanut had begun to suspect it was not real. She had seen many of the Agar suffer at the hands of Arabs in Aweil and yet they never used their supposed powers. Why not just eat the oppressors at night if they could?

Bol turned sharply, accidentally stepping on a rusted iron sheet by the roadside. The cracking sound brought Nyanut out of her reverie just in time to see Bol leaving the road and stepping into the forest. She fell in behind him now that they were in the forest.

The old familiar sound of birds and insects chirping welcomed them. It had been two years since she last heard such sounds. Tears welled in her eyes as the wild music made its way to her heart and her soul. The music always hit something in her, something too mysterious to only be her heart. So, she had borrowed the Christian term, soul.

Bol continued walking. A monkey stood on its hind legs and watched them from a nearby tree. It jumped down and made noise. Other monkeys climbed down from nearby trees. *It called them*, Nyanut realized. Bol tried to shoo then away but they just kept coming. Nyanut shook, frightened. The monkeys closed in. Bol kept moving and motioned her to follow. He stopped in a nearby thicket and removed something. The monkeys scattered, running back to climb trees.

Bol slung the gun on his shoulder. *They fear guns*. Nyanut watched the monkeys, amazed at their likeness to human beings. She watched the gun too, amazed. Bol had a gun. That means he has met the SPLA. Her hope flared up.

After a lot of twists and turns in the jungle, Nyanut heard sounds and thereafter, saw people moving. A camp. Most people she could see were young men, but there was also an older man here and there.

Bol moved steadily towards an older man who sat on stone leaning against a tree. Many other men sat around him. Most of them had guns. Bol stood attention and saluted.

"I've brought her Captain," Bol said

"I can see," the Captain said, "I hope she is as strong as you made me believe." He inspected Nyanut, gazing at her with piercing eyes. His eyes lingered at parts of her body, as if she were naked. Nyanut shuddered.

"Kon Lual," the Captain said, extending his hand to Nyanut. Nyanut shook it, uncertain

"Bakhita Nyanut Garang," she said, hoping it was the right thing to say.

"We've waited here a couple days more than we'd have loved to. Bol made us believe we had a very valuable fighter in town we shouldn't leave behind." Nyanut glanced at Bol gratefully, he was beyond earshot, sharing a plate of food with a sentry. She said nothing, just looked to the ground, fidgeting with her hands.

"And I hope you cook well. I haven't tasted a woman's food in a longtime," Another man who sat next to the Captain said. The entire gathering laughed. Only Nyanut didn't, she didn't see anything funny.

"Dut, take her to Old man," the Captain ordered a young man. Dut stood up and motioned for Nyanut to follow. He walked ahead humming Piny Ci Deng Nok under his breath. He carried no gun. Guns were few here, and Nyanut had noticed that.

The young man didn't say anything by way of conversation to Nyanut. He just moved as if she did not exist. They reached a thicket that looked like an improvised shelter. Logs laid neatly on sacks placed on a canopy.

"Old man, see what I've brought for you. A helper! A girl" Dut said innocently

There was a rustle from inside the shelter and a muscular old woman emerged wearing green Khaki complete with a cap.

"Where's she?" She asked, voice deep. Old man.

Nyanut laughed despite herself.

CHAPTER 7

***

Alor Biong moved stealthily along the shores of the river Kiir, ducking low from time to time. He was on duty today. It was his turn to watch for danger that may surprise the crew. It had been two weeks since his arrival from Abyei town and didn't miss it. He loved it here in Kiirkou, if only because he was almost beyond Arab humiliation. Almost because the Messirya still brought their cows as far as the river Kiir, accompanied by their heavily armed mobile force. Alor was on the lookout for them now.

It was early morning. Dew dripped from the tree leaves and birds twittered, excited for the new day. Thick fog hang on the riverbanks, and Alor moved as quietly as he could. He carried no gun; they hadn't taught him how to use one yet. The few guns available were for those who knew how to use them. So, Alor only carried a machete. His clothes were damp and soaked in dew, but he felt surprisingly good. The knowledge that he was doing something the Arabs didn't want him doing was good. He wanted to hurt them. They acted like they were immortal in Abyei town and Alor intended to show them here in Kiirkou, all men are mortal.

A lone Messirya rider appeared on the banks of the river, and Alor almost jumped. The meaning of such an appearance wasn't pleasant, because it implied that the very people you spied on could also easily spy on you. Alor looked around nervously. His young eyes did not spot a second rider. *A scout then*. The crew commander had promised to get him a gun if he could spot a lone armed Arab. Alor had been on the lookout every time he was on sentry duty. And his chance had come today. He ducked lower and executed a prearranged signal, a hoot like an owl. Owls were rare in the forests of Kiirkou, but they trusted that the Arabs wouldn't know this.

Alor cupped his hands and brought them to his mouth and produced a perfect hooting sound. Even a hunter wouldn't have been able to tell that the sound had come from a man and not from the bird. He made the sound twice and waited, restless, fearing that the lone raider would disappear, and this became another lost opportunity. *Come on*. The reply was taking longer than usual. Alor peeped out from the undergrowth where he hid. The lone rider was still there, glancing around nervously while his horse drank from the river. The reply came in two bursts, perfect. Only the leader of the crew would do this, his uncle Kuol. Alor was glad he had not sent anyone and came to do the task himself. He was the sharpest shooter they had.

There was a disturbance in the undergrowth under one of the trees nearby and Alor hid, just a precaution in case another Messirya scout should turn up this way. Captain Kuol surfaced from the undergrowth. He made gestures to Alor to show him where the enemy he had spotted was. Alor pointed with his hand without leaving his hiding place. Captain Kuol then fell into position and aimed at the unsuspecting Arab scout. Alor watched him, praying silently that he didn't miss even though Alor knew well that the Captain was a sharpshooter.

***

Captain Kuol slid down belly first and aimed at the Messirya rider's head. *Don't miss.* Slowly, he brought his hand to the trigger and fingered it. He hesitated a bit. Taking a man's life still unsettled him even though he had taken more than a dozen lives already. It just didn't feel right, even though he knew he did it for the greater good and the trigger felt strangely cold. He hesitated for another heartbeat, wishing the Messirya would ride away. He didn't.

Captain Kuol pulled the trigger and felt the bullet hit the man before the sound of the gunshot spread in the forest, echoing. Not even the murmuring of nature could subdue the sound. The rider fell and his horse ran.

"Get the gun quickly," the Captain said

"Yes, sir!" Alor replied and ran off

The Captain maintained his position, gun readily aimed as cover for Alor just in case a second rider should hear the gunshot and come to help. The lad came back carrying the gun clumsily. The Captain quickly removed the magazine and emptied the gun of any bullets that might be in muzzle then handed it back to Alor. All this was done under a minute.

Any gunshot in Kiirkou was always too loud given the dense forest. All their operations thus depended upon haste. They ran for it, making no effort to cover their tracks as it was no good in the wet ground. They wouldn't go to their base yet; it was one of the codes of the bandits of Kiirkou. The Messirya should never know their hideout even if it meant the death of the one being pursued, he must first run and lead the pursuer in the wrong direction. They kept running. After a while, Captain Kuol stopped and put his hand up in a military style gesture. Alor stopped beside him.

The Captain seemed attentive. He listened with well-trained

ears, sharpened by years of training himself to listen. Survival as an outlaw required a lot of listening, any little sounds ignored could lead to death. They were always being hunted. The Captain visibly concentrated.

"We are being followed," he said, still listening, "A rider, possibly two. Even more. So, we should run in water, they are a bit far off. They are following our tracks but not our sounds. They can't hear us."

The two men ran, splashing through water and skipping muddy spots only to step into the next pool of water. The Captain put up his right hand again and rolled it into a fist. Alor stopped.

"We climb this tree," the Captain said, pointing at a tree that stood in a pool of water, the trunk mostly submerged. Both men climbed up and waited, having hidden themselves securely under the leaves. They heard splashes of water shortly afterwards and somebody cursed in Arabic.

"Confound the Jenge!" a voice said.

"They grow bolder by each passing day." A second voice said.

"If only they would stop and face us." The first voice said.

"They will do no such thing. They know they only strive with guerrilla tactics given their inferior weaponry. "

"You wonder who teaches these Jenge guerrilla tactics."

"The Western missionaries of course, pretending to preach religion while in reality they prepare savages for a revolution."

"We'll have to talk Colonel Yasin Mohammed into bringing his forces this way – sshhh." The first voice cautioned.

Captain Kuol barely stopped himself from cocking his gun. He peered through the leaves. He could just make out an outline of what looked like two riders, the fog still hung thick. They weren't moving in their direction. Something had drawn their attention. The two riders turned their horses to the opposite direction and galloped off.

They waited in their hiding place. Part of being a successful bandit was learning to take everything for a ruse. They suspected that this abrupt retreat was intended to make them feel secure and to lure them out of hiding. They waited for a long time after the riders had left, then came out of hiding. Captain Kuol released a sigh of relief. *Still alive.* He glanced at Alor who still hugged a branch tight.

"Cheer up little man," Captain Kuol said, "The worst is yet to come."

The two men climbed down and began their long meandering journey to the base. Nobody went to the base directly. You had to meander. This sometimes involved moving around the base several times until you were sure you weren't being followed.

The two men entered the base an hour later, exhausted to the bone, but they had something to show for their efforts, a gun. An extra gun was always welcome here. The crew cheered when they saw the gun. Everybody seemed happy to see their Captain back safely. They wanted him to have an escort wherever he went but the Captain would have none of that.

"We'll have enough time for such military shows once in Bilpam," the Captain always said.

Amidst all the happiness, the one man was happiest to see the Captain return safely was Sergeant Rou. He was a short man, thickly built with a barely visible moustache. He saluted the Captain. A sign that the command had reverted to the most senior present, Captain Kuol. The Captain liked his deputy. He could understand why the sergeant was so eager to give up command. Controlling the bandits was no easy work.

* * *

The crew stood attention in a military style parade. Twelve strong excluding their Captain. Most were young men, but old men were there too. The Arabs pushed everybody to the breaking point. Those who broke stayed serving them forever. Those who didn't either escaped to areas beyond their reach or ran to the bush to start a resistance.

"Attention men!" the Captain's voice boomed. "We'll leave base for a few days. It's time you train to be physically fit, or I won't make it to Bilpalm with this sorry lot."

CHAPTER 8

The thirteen marched back to base, exhausted. Ten continuous days of doing all manner of physical excersise, and running long distances, had made them more exhausted than strong. Alor Biong marched, his meagre belongings tied to his back in an improvised blue sack bag. He felt very weak, but Captain Kuol had said that as they exercised continuously, their bodies would learn to endure the fatigue longer. Alor believed him, but his body complained.

They marched quietly. Quietness was their number one code. Just like people keep quiet at gatherings so that nobody takes note of them, the bandits of Kiirkou believed that the Arabs wouldn't take note of them if they were quiet. For a time at least. Only the sound of a gun was a necessary noise. So, they marched in a single file. Not bothering to send scouts ahead. They were in the part of the forest they deemed safe enough.

They reached camp at last, having encountered nothing save for the murmuring of nature. Even the well-trained ears of Captain Kuol heard nothing out of the ordinary. They entered base at noon, in high spirits. Alor Biong wanted to just lie down and sleep, but that would happen in his previous life. Now he was a bandit and he offered to be on first watch while others took a nap.

* * *

Captain Kuol sat cleaning his gun. He felt tired but a leader must be strong for his crew. The boys were taking a nap. Let them. He had allowed them to, at least this once. He frowned, *why did he feel so worried?* Since his arrival at the base, he had felt a sense of foreboding. He kept cleaning his gun. It *could be the fatique*, he thought but he looked around base just in case. Nothing had changed, the base was the same. He began putting his gun together part after part. All that trouble just so you could kill a man smoothly.

Something is wrong. He moved inspecting the little shelters. Everything was in place. He moved around camp, inspecting. He froze, there was a big shallow hole in in the ground, covered with branches.

He lifted the branches, following them until it disappeared some distance away in an undergrowth out of the base, where the ground was strong even in heavy downpours. *Could we have made this?* He followed it back to camp. Just outside the camp, he stopped. *What's this?* He bent down to inspect. It was a mark of a horse hoof.

"Shit," Captain Kuol swore and began to run towards camp.

"Captain," Alor Biong said, running alongside him, "what is it?"

"Death," the Captain said.

"Move camp!" he commanded. The rest of the crew who had been taking a nap woke up panic stricken.

Kalashnikovs began to scream from the trees nearby. Captain

Kuol watched the crew take cover. Only seven of them had guns, the rest trusted their comrades to aid their escape. *Damn it.* He lifted his gun.

"March towards Abiemnom," he screamed, and the boys scrambled through the thicket. The first member of the crew fell, expected but no less painful. Two of the crew members turned to help their fallen comrade.

"Keep moving you dummies! He's dead," The Captain bellowed. The two men turned and ran. Captain Kuol and those with guns covered them.

Captain Kuol knew enough to concentrate on a retreat. They had been ambushed at their own base and more than that, the crew only had eight armed men. They were against about four times their number. The Captain sighed. Terrible odds. He breathed in and out. The rest of the seven armed divided themselves each behind a tree. They had basic shooting skills. Only sergeant Rou was close to being a sharpshooter.

The Captain aimed at an exposed Arab. The crew said he was sharpshooter, and he knew he could hit more targets than most. Though a sharpshooter did not miss, so he was no sharpshooter. He pulled the trigger and felt the bullet hit the target.

He had known this feeling since he was a boy when he had shot birds with a catapult years ago. It was a feeling in his arms, like he had just punched a mattress.

"Orderly retreat," the Captain bellowed, "Alor, cover me."

The lad had learnt to shoot recently, not well enough, but he knew to cock a gun and fire. Another crew member fell. An armed one. *Two.* Captain Kuol found himself counting in his head as the bandits of Kiirkou were being exterminated.

* * *

Sergeant Rou ducked behind a tree and slid into the thick under-growth while trying to cover his comrades. Two of the crew had fallen. True, he had chosen to be an outlaw. He had known the price but that didn't make it less a surprise when the time of payment came. Two good men lost. Why the hell hadn't they just made for Bilpam. He aimed and shot. A man screamed and fell. He aimed and shot again. A man screamed but stood on his feet, injured but not dead.

They had mistreated him in Omdurman, these Arabs. They had had him beaten, forced to join the army and sent to the frontline so he could die quickly. All because he dared to love Fatima, he, a mere Southern boy. They had tortured him mercilessly, even broke his ribs, the bastards. He stood up and began to shoot, screaming obscenities.

* * *

Alor Biong felt the bullet hit the target. For the first since the fight had started, he felt surprisingly thrilled. He had shot a man, no, a monster. It was hard for him to imagine these Arabs as men. He shot again, not bothering to aim considering how bad he was at hitting the target. Images swarm before him, Ngok executed by firing squad at the shores of the Nyamora. *What's that?*

Someone screamed,

"Miith aguech- sons of bitches!" Alor looked around to see the speaker. Sergeant Rou stood, screaming and shooting at anything that looked like a messirya hideout. His insults followed the bullets. *Madness.* Alor tried to run to him, to pull him back behind the tree. He stopped. There were less gunshots than before and the messirya were retreating. Alor screamed too and began to shoot sporadically. The rest of the armed and the unarmed crew members followed suit. Morale was high, they had won. It was only Captain Kuol who didn't join them. He stayed, crouching and shooting. One, two then three of the retreating Messirya fell.

The survivors ran pell-mell through the forest, but the bandits did not pursue, instead turning to inspect the damage. Two men had fallen and another two were injured. Alor looked at the fallen, tears in his eyes. He knew both men well, though he had only been with them for a month. Deng Akonon and Kur Rou were men the whole crew had relied on. Deng Akonon cooked the tastiest meals Alor had ever tasted. Kur Rou knew almost every herb in the forest and the diseases it cured. Their knowledge was lost forever now.

They dug a quick grave and placed the two men in, then filled the holes, after singing Piny Ci Deng Nok. No one offered words for the dead. It was all quiet. The birds sang and hot tears dropped from Alor's eyes.

***

Sergeant Rou attended to one of the wounded, he had a broken arm, or at least that is what the victim said.

He cleaned the bleeding area and massaged it, searching for any broken bone using the famous inherited talent of the Pan Rou clan. The bullet had passed cleanly through flesh, miraculously avoiding the bones.

"It's alright Koch," he said patting the wounded man on the back, "just a wound."

Koch tried to smile but only grimaced with pain.

He moved on. The next person had a more serious injury, he was shot through the leg. The bullet had missed the bones but had torn a muscle. He bandaged it with a torn cloth.

"You'll walk in a few days," he told the man.

Captain Kuol motioned to him to come. Sergeant Rou approached his Captain who sat further away, thinking as always.

* * *

Captain Kuol watched him approach. He liked his sergeant and yet he had seen something in this man today, something new, and he had to confirm it. He watched the sargent, concentrating mostly on the magazines around the man's waist. *Unless my eyes have played tricks on me.*

He raised an eyebrow. The magazines on the Sergeant's waist were ripped in places, shot at, and yet not a bullet hit him.

"Sir!" The Sergeant said, standing to attention and saluting. Captain Kuol moved towards him and prodded the holes in the magazines with his index finger. Sergeant Rou looked down at his waist, eyes wide.

"Interesting," The Captain said.

"We move. Towards Abiemnom."

CHAPTER 9

The forest was thick and seemed to go on forever. They had been moving in it since dawn and it was now almost sun set, and there was no end to the forest in sight. Nyanut sighed. *No wonder they call it rol chuol akol*, she thought, *the forest of sunset*. The sun changed colour. From yellow to deep orange, the colour of a glowing splint. It sunk slowly until it disappeared down the horizon. She shivered. The men in her company had told stories of man eaters in this region, she didn't believe them of course, but the dark forest seemed alive.

Fires became visible from a distance signalling a settlement. That would be Cueibet, the place Old man had told her about. Aker Deng was the name of the kindly woman and despite her looks, Nyanut had found no fault in her. After spending almost two months Nyanut saw her muscular body less as threatening, and more as normal. She knew almost every town they passed through.

So far, every town they had passed had an appalling country-side. The gardens lay desolate even though it was May, grannaries had been burnt down, and the starving citizens lay dying in the in open country. Only the towns were left alive, somewhat stocked with food. The countryside around Wau town had been even worse because the Fertit pro government militias had wrecked havoc on the starving Dinka. That always annoyed Nyanut. She hadn't been able to figure out what made people turn on their own and she hoped the story was not the same in Cueibet.

The crew stopped for the night. They would not enter Cueibet. Only Nyanut and Old man would. The Sudan Armed Forces did not feel threatened by women, not even abnormally muscular ones like Aker Deng.

Captain Kon Lual posted sentries, and the crew lay down to rest. Strictly no fire was allowed lest the government forces spot them. The men conversed cheerfully. That surprised Nyanut. Where did hunted men find that happiness?

Aker Deng took her aside.

"We'll enter town early tomorrow," She said, "but be cautious for this is the territory we have grown up being afraid of. It might be nothing but be weary anyway because it defies logic that people would create so many tales out of nothing."

Nyanut slept uneasily that night. She dreamt she was back in Makom village. Makom was intact and everyone she knew was there. She had gone to fetch firewood with her agemates and were just returning home in the evening when one of the girls tapped her on the shoulder and said in a whisper,

"That is Mamer Khaman the Agaar man's house. Let's pass this way instead." she showed Nyanut a different path, but Nyanut was adamant.

"Fear will kill you one day," she said, "why hasn't he eaten anyone in all these years he's been in Makom?"

The other girls looked at her long and hard.

"Those who say they've never seen a lion will meet it one day." The eldest of them said. The girls followed the other footpath until the last of them had gone. Nyanut's hair stood on end.

Shadows took on sinister shapes and she ran with firewood on her head. She heard footsteps behind her, but she did not turn. If she turned, she knew she would lose the firewood.

She steadied her nerves and moved but for every step she took, there was a corresponding step taken by someone behind her. She had almost made it home when a cold hand touched her back. Her fear gave way and she screamed.

Aker Deng covered her mouth and Nyanut struggled, writhing where she slept until her eyes fluttered open, and she realized where she was.

* * *

When they entered Cueibet the following morning, the town was no different from the towns they had passed so far. Hungry children watched with their telltale pot bellies caused by dire malnutrition. Nyanut noticed that the people of Cueibet were even more nomadic than her Aweil people. People cultivated on a small scale. Many were contented with milk as their staple food.

There was a small army garrison in the area otherwise, the people of Cueibet mostly did as they pleased. Nyanut took it all in and wondered how people who were said to be man eaters starved while there were healthy Arabs in town with them. She shuddered at the thought of it.

Aker Deng did not mind the people of Cueibet because her eyes were only for the military aspect of the town, looking for something to report back to Captain Kon Lual.

"Stop looking at them like that. People get suspicious when

you stare at them," she scolded Nyanut when she caught her staring at people in the small market of Cueibet with wide eyes. The two bought some milk and did a quick survey of the town before going back to base.

"The way is clear, Captain," Aker Deng said to Captain Kon once back at the base, "there's a small army garrison in town but we can dodge that one successfully."

Captain Kon thought for a while, smacking his lips and looking at the maps laid out on the ground before him.

"Next is Rumbek," he said, "we move there next. Now."

Nyanut, young and new to this habit of moving such long distances within such a short time collapsed on hearing that the crew was about to move again. Aker Deng became alarmed and sprinkled water in her face. She came to briefly, before blacking out again.

"I'll have to carry her," Aker Deng aka Old man informed the rest of them, and she threw Nyanut over her back and began to move. Some of the men watched her with nothing less than admiration.

PART TWO

THE ROAD
TO BILPAM

CHAPTER 10

It had begun again in earnest, not in the middle, but from the beginning. This was a very familiar cycle and Yusif Doka had seen it twice. First at the Torit mutiny, then at the Anyanya one and he had been deeply involved in both. Doka had known that it would come again for cycles have no end. Yet now that it was here, the fore knowledge didn't help him much, this was the cycle of hate and it had only two sides. The Northernern and Southernern side. It was the kind of cycle that matured in agreements and started over again at their dishonouring.

He thought hard because he had to decide quickly. He paced up and down in his compound at the outskirts of Yambio town. *Dammit this should be easy*, he thought. It was not though.

True, it could be easy for him to continue living as if nothing had happened, but the politics of Sudan did not require neutrality. You were either Northern or Southern, anything inbetween was worse because either side would think you worked for the other. The only neutrals stayed abroad. He, Doka could not go abroad. If he took refuge in a neighbouring country, they would get him like they got Father Saturnino Lohure in the 1960s. The Sudanese regimes did not forget a leader easily, much less if he ever controlled an army of his own. Yusif Doka, a former Anyanya commander, did not doubt that someone might be at the army headquarters in Khartoum asking for his head.

Think, think. He kept pacing. He did not doubt that soon enough, someone would be sent to him to talk about the possibility of his being put on active army duty. He wanted to be gone then or ready to join by the time the regime thought to ask for his services. Refusal would be akin to suicide. He had to weigh up the pros and cons of his eventual choice he needed to talk to someone. *But who?* The junior officers that had been under his command as Anyanya forces were in various parts of the country though some were in Yambio town. He had to talk to them or one of them at least.

He made his way to the house of his former lieutenant, who now commanded a platoon in Torit, but was in Yambio on a short leave. If he was going to make his way to Bilpam, Doka decided he wanted to have someone like Kwaje by his side. True, this was a common cause for all Southenters, but things could quickly change. If that happened, he needed to have men he could trust not to be turncoats, the kind of men who could identify more in with him than merely being Southerners. Azande men.

* * *

"General Doka," Lieutenant Kwaje saluted.

"Ah Lieutenant Kwaje. That was a lifetime ago. Now I am just citizen Doka. "

"Retired or not, you're still my General. I'm glad you came; I had wanted to visit you for a while." Doka met Lieutenant Kwaje 's eyes and both smiled. They could read each other. That's why they had been friends in the first place.

"I hope you are not thinking of retiring," Doka said, taking a chair and sitting. Lieutenant Kwaje sat after he had.

"Nothing of the sort General. I'm merely alarmed at what is happening in Upper Nile. "

"Ah, Upper Nile yes, that's rather serious, but you've got nothing to fear. You're on the winning side. "

"So it may seem," said Lieutenant Kwaje, visibly thinking, "but military intelligence said that the SPLA receives no less than a hundred volunteer recruits on a bad day. Close to a thousand on a good day most of whom are Dinka and Nuer. Smaller tribes like Shiluk and Bari too. If they lose, fine but what if the Southerners win this time round General? What will the Azande be? "

"We'll be cowards who collaborated with the Northerners and live in shame forever, Lieutenant," Doka said, whispering.

"We have to find a way out of it General. Down in Torit, Northern officers have began spying on us. I can't work with people who may look for the slightest provocation to give me to the firing squad. I've already decided to throw in my lot with the SPLA. I've only come to ask you to for your opinion."

Yusif Doka smiled and gripped Lieutenant Kwaje's shoulder.

"I too have come to ask for your opinion Lieutenant. Gather the boys. We'll start for Bilpam tomorrow. The Azande warriors will not be left behind."

Having arrived at a decision, citizen Doka, who now found himself a General for the second time, had a lot to plan in a single night. First was his family and how to best get them out of harm's way. Harm that was sure to befall them because of his actions. Junior officers' families might not be located but a General's could be located as sure the Nile River flows North. The other things included logistics for the new army, and the roads they would take to avoid Sudan Armed Forces ambushes.

That afternoon, General Doka hired a small truck to take his family to the border of the Democratic Republic of Congo to 'visit relatives'. From there, they would cross the border into the Congolese border town of Doruma. They took just a fraction of their belongings so as not to arouse suspicion. As soon as the family were on their way, Doka took out maps that he had used in his previous stint as a General. They were Sudanese maps detailing footpaths, military garrisons and both major and minor towns. For the rest of the day and into the night, he traced a footpath with his fingers using a kerosene lamp for light.

He was good at sketching maps. His education was minimal, having reached senior three, but was then expelled from Rumbek secondary school for taking part in a student protest. Despite this, his skill was superior to most of his educated colleagues' when it came to practical tasks. He didn't sleep that night, not for want of trying, though it was his long-standing belief that a General didn't sleep until he saw a mission through.

When a knock came at the door at midnight, it found General Doka awake tracing footpaths on the map, though he had already found the safest footpath to use. He stopped and opened the door a crack and peeped out.

"General," Lieutenant Kwaje whispered, and General Doka opened the door wider without a word for the lieutenant to enter. Two other men stumbled in after him and General Doka slammed the door shut after peering into the black night with his well-trained eyes.

"How many, Lieutenant?"

"Twenty-four, General. Those I could trust."

"Good. That's two full platoons, armed. "

"General, the men are for wrecking havoc on the commissioner's residence before we move on."

"What? What kind of fool's errand is that? I'm the commander here now lieutenant, you made me your General. You want us chased all the way to Bilpam? How many of us could survive such a chase, do you think? "

The lieutenant kept quiet and General Doka walked towards the maps, motioning him to come over. Lieutenant Kwaje stood over the maps with his general.

"This," General Doka said, tracing a blue line on the map which zizagged around a host of towns and eventually ending in Kapoeta, "is the route we are taking. It'll take us safely as far as Kapoeta. After that, we will either sneak around the town or pass through with a little shoot out." The lieutenant nodded.

General Doka glanced at his watch. It was one o'clock in the morning. He folded the maps and stuffed them into a small bag, it was the only one he was going to carry on the journey.

"We move," he said.

One of the other two soldiers who came with lieutenant Kwaje picked up the General's small bag and all four walked quietly into the night.

* * *

The boys were waiting in a hideout near Maridi road. General Doka spent the time walking to the hideout, thinking. To him, thinking was a necessary ritual when performing a task. Many do not know how to think because if something great just crosses your mind while you're doing something else, that's not thinking.

General Doka concentrated. He was leading two platoons on a journey of hundreds of miles through regime-controlled territories.

How do I do it? If he divided the two platoons between himself and his Lieutenant, moving along different routes, it would be safer. That wasn't practical though, because the only close to safe route was the one General Doka knew from tracing it onto the map and moving separately would greatly reduce their firepower if any of the platoons came under attack.

Thunder rumbled and lightning flashed across the sky. General Doka looked up. *Are the Zandi ancestors cursing or blessing us?* He didn't pretend to hear an answer. He jogged lightly and the others did likewise until they reached Maridi road. It hadn't rained yet, but the wind was blowing hard. The green trees swayed as dark masses in the night. It was a risky night to escape into the jungle, but general Doka couldn't change the weather. That was the nature of this cycle. It sucked people in. The Arabs hated you and because they hate you, you would hate them too. That would infuriate them, and they would kill you or your kind, and you, in turn, would hit back and kill them. The collaborators had to kill their own kind, and, in the cycle, such people would be labelled Northerners.

The twenty-four stood at attention before General Doka, as a dark mass of eyes twinkling in the night.

"A revolution, " General Doka said, addressing his men, "begins with a single step. This step has always been metaphorical but it's literal for us today, and now in particular. You can hear the rumbling thunder and see the flashes of lightning. We need to beat the rain so that by the time it is muddy enough for our boots to leave prints, we shall be on the rarely used footpath already."

Even as the General talked, it began to drizzle. The General stopped and lieutenant Kwaje picked up.

"Now, we match fearlessly towards freedom or death!" The

lieutenant bellowed, and the men raised up their weapons in salute. Without a word, the march began. Each man jogged in an orderly manner, trusting in the rumble of thunder to mask the sound of their feet.

CHAPTER 11

"Can it be true, or has the great tale creation of Mading Aweil made it's way to Equatoria?" Captain asked Bol and Dut. The two had recently started sneaking into towns instead of Nyanut and Aker Deng aka Old man. Dinka men were not uncommon in Equatoria, but women were. Thus, sending men in would be less likely to raise suspicion.

"We cannot verify the authenticity of the information Captain, but so far, we have heard the same story from five different people."

"And the commissioner does this every Moday evening? "

"Yes, Captain. "

"I'll have to go on Monday. I want to see this for myself. "

Nyanut listened to the Captain and the two scouts, interested but tired. They had been travelling for over two months, dodging between towns until they had arrived to Kapoeta. As well as fatigue, the crew had lost a lot of people. Originally thirty, the crew now had only seventeen.

Bakhita Nyanut watched the trees around the camp. This forest was much thicker than the ones she had seen in Bahrelghazel. The rains never seemed to stop in this side of the country. IIt had been a month since they entered Equatoria, Nyanut could swear that it had been raining every two days since. Captain Kon had told her that they called it Equatoria for a reason but what that reason was, he did not clarify. Nyanut did not understand Captain Kon Lual. He talked patriotism and acted most of it but to Nyanut, he was no better than Master Abdallah, if not worse. Everyone in the crew knew what went on between her and the captain every night, a replica of her exact ordeal with Master Abdallah, but nobody could do anything about it, not even old man.

Nyanut sighed. What had she expected? That because the Northerners mistreated the Southerners, the Southerners would somehow form one big family? She should have known better. This was the nature of life. Those who had power could have their way no matter who gave them that power. It didn't matter whether they were black or brown, Southern or Northern. She tucked that lesson away finding she was learning rather quickly these days.

Even Bol, the one she had trusted for so long did not stand up for her. Nyanut had made a mistake thinking Bol would somehow fill the shoes of her brother Yel.

Nyanut wanted to go into the town when Captain Kon Lual and the scouts went the following morning. That night, she played the tried and tested methods of womanly control. She cooperated fully and the captain was impressed. She just had to press him a little to take her with him into the town and he accepted as she had expected him to.

* * *

Morning came, and the four started for the town as dawn was a few hours to break. They moved swiftly in the semi-darkness. They could see enough but not too much, passing empty homesteads where inhabitants still lay asleep. They hid in thickets near what was said to be the commissioner's practice square so by the time dawn broke the four had good view as they waited. They heard a truck and ducked lower into the thickets.

A green military truck came into sight. Nyanut counted as soldiers jumped down. Twenty-one soldiers.

"The District Commissioner," The captain whispered.

The District Commissioner moved majestically and accepted a weapon from an officer who held it out to him.

"A 9mm Patchett submachine gun," Captain Kon whispered, "the deadliest weapon I have held."

The commissioner waved to the soldiers who stood, their guns pointed at rugged handcuffed men who started to jump down from the truck one after another. Six. Nyanut counted. These men were prisoners because they bore the telltale marks, the wounds, the filth. It was all there, just the same things she had seen in Aweil. These were obviously Southerners.

The Commissioner cocked his weapon and waited as his soldiers tied each prisoner to a tree. Meanwhile another truck arrived, bringing soldiers who jumped down while the truck moved and took positions all over the square, coming dangerously close to where the four hid. Nyanut remembered the rosary that hung from her neck for the first time in months and held it.

The Commissioner aimed at one of the prisoners and shot. He missed, smiled, and shot another. That missed too. He let that prisoner be, and shot at the second, the bullet hit prisoner's head and he screamed. His soldiers saluted. A target practice, Nyanut realised. The lucky ones who were missed twice survived to see the following Monday practice. Nyanut saw no fear on the prisoners' faces. They were resigned to their fate. The commissioner hit three of the six lined before him. His soldiers carried the dead and threw them into the bush. The lucky three were whipped as they clambered aboard the military truck again. The two trucks' engines roared back to life and the trucks rolled away.

"Shit!" Captain Kon Lual swore loudly when the trucks had gone. The four came out of their hideout slowly, one at a time. First to come out was Bol who crouched down on all fours and put his ear close to the ground and listened attentively. He motioned to Dut to come out and the rest followed.

* * *

"The county seems to be armed to the teeth. Armed men are teeming everywhere," General Doka said to Liutenant Kwaje. "We might have to shoot our way through if we want to proceed with the original plan."

Lieutenant Kwaje smiled.

"What other choice have we? Throw our hands up in the air and and tell the district commissioner we have changed our minds about going to Bilpam?" Both men looked at each other and laughed.

The general and his lieutenant kept pacing around their base. The men were orderly, former military men all of them. Some cleaned guns while others dug holes to make fires and roast wild meat.

The two leaders of the Yambio group were still pacing up and down, when a sentry came to report.

"General, we have spotted three armed Southerners and a girl. They are making for that village at the outskirts of the forest."

"Bring them to the base, alive" General Doka said, "We will find out what their motives are."

"Yes, sir."

* * *

The Captain and his small group moved through the forest; weapons slung on their backs.

"Sabit- stand still," A voice said in the bushes. The three-armed men instinctively reached for their guns but before they could hold them in shooting position, armed men emerged from the trees on opposite sides of the footpath they had been following and formed a ring. Captain Kon Lual sighed, resigned to the fate that surely awaited them.

"Drop your guns," Said one of the armed men who appeared to be the leader. Captain Kon Lual and Dut dropped their guns, but Bol Deng held on.

"Drop it before you get us killed" The Captain hissed. Bol held on and a gun butt hit him at the back of his head causing him to fall, unconscious. The armed men collected the guns and marched the captives away, the unconscious Bol carried like a sack of flour on one of the men's shoulders.

* * *

The smell of roast bush meat penetrated Nyanut's nostrils, and it only became stronger as they marched towards base. Nyanut salivated, although she knew the journey to that base was probably the last, she would ever make.

They reached the base and before Nyanut could even adjust her eyes to take in her surroundings, "My, God! If this is not the lion of Immatong," Captain Kon Lual exclaimed.

General Doka stopped short of taking another bite from the rabbit thigh he was dealing with and shaded his eyes with his left hand to have a clear look at the speaker.

"Interesting. What might a great Captain like yourself be doing in the bushes of Equatoria? Last I heard, you were stationed in port Sudan."

"That's old information, General. I deserted about a year ago."

"Where might you be heading with these sorry lot," said General Doka, pointing at the Captain's campanions. The Captain hesitated.

"Bilpam," Nyanut said without thinking

"Excellent." General Doka said, watching Nyanut with interest. A frail looking little girl with loads of courage.

"Guns down, men. The road to Bilpam is a perilous one and one can never too many companions for such a journey."

CHAPTER 12

They moved in a single file never stopping, never out of breath, like robots. Alor Biong had known ever since he was seven that someday, he would die. He had cried the day he found out that man must die. First, he was reckless with his life, after all, he must lose it someday. As time went on, he realized that death was part of the beauty of life. As the bandits of Kiirkou moved through the forests towards Abiemnom, and seeing how the men never got tired in their efforts to escape death, Alor Biong was convinced that what he had thought for so long was true for all men. Everyone fancies immortality even with he knowledge that such a thing is impossible.

"Halt!" Captain Kuol commanded. The bandits came to an abrupt stop. They had been moving for over a fortnight with very little rest, zigzagging their way through the forest. Alor Biong watched the Captain. He had a haggard look that was uncharacteristic. The Captain may at times have looked thoughtful but not haggard. The ambush, Alor thought, it had taken its toll on him.

"We camp here to recover our strength. The worst is behind us,

77

let's get ready to face that which might meet us in Abiemnom," Captain Kuol added. The crew chose a thicket under a dense canopy for a camp.

As soon as they had chosen the campsite, Alor Biong, like the rest of the crew, could not resist the urge to sleep. They shoved aside their belongings and lay down on the wet ground under a canopy, forgetting their troubles for the moment. Captain Kuol did not so much as wink but kept a straight posture and took position as a sentry even though it was against protocol; for junior officers are to guard their seniors, not the other way round.

* * *

Captain Kuol watched over the men he was leading to Bilpam. They were very weak men, but he didn't blame them. Sucessfully fighting off fatigue required a lot of practice. These young men had just gotten started. They will learn once we reach Bilpam, Captain Kuol thought. He sighed. He had deliberately avioded thinking about the journey. Crossing the Nuer and Shilluk lands was an ordeal he dreaded. Abiemnom was just three miles away and beyond it lay the the Nuer and Shilluk lands controlled by the Anyanya ll. He had crossed these very lands a year ago with Captain Bagak Aguek. He, Kuol had been a noncommissioned officer back then. The brutality and the knowledge of what was being done to them by fellow Southerners was hard to forget.

* * *

Kuol Deng moved through Noong village of central Abyei, just one of the many sons of the late chief. Twelve years later and people still spoke of his father like he was alive.

Kuol had been only six when his father died. He had seen his father, and yet he could hardly remember what the man looked like.

It was a clear morning and as he strolled on through the village as he passed people going about their businesses in their homesteads.

"Salaam aleikum-peace be with you," he greeted as he passed each homestead. He spoke Arabic most of the time, it was the language he grew up speaking.

He continued through the village. It was the middle of April, so he was going to visit his garden and do some clearing, because the rains were approaching soon. He was eighteen and enjoyed the respect that came with being the late great paramount chief's son and a brother to the current chief, but the benefits ended there. He had to work for his own bread since he was one of the youngest sons at the time of his father's death. The older sons had some inheritance but not the younger ones. No matter how wealthy the man was, he couldn't leave inheritance for each of his more than fourty sons. Once the old man was gone, the only thing the young sons had was the advice to go to school and get an education.

The fact that Arabs were the teachers in most Abyei schools ensured that Kuol and other young men, with their characteristic Jieng pride, dropped out. When Kuol had dropped, he'd tried to concentrate on his farm but even there, he was not beyond Arab humiliation. An occassional Messirya preteneded not to have seen the garden and grazed his cows there. Many times, he had already contemplated going to join the SPLA but each time, the elders dissuaded him for his brother's actions had already cost the family four of its prominent members.

He reached the garden and commenced his work. In less than a year from now, he would marry, and any man who wanted a wife had to have properties he called his own, earned through his own sweat. He cleared most of the garden and burnt the bushes.

He was still working on the garden when the worst Messirya attack on Noong took place.

The sound of the Kalashnikov rifles, the screams of children, and the mooing of cows filled the air. Kuol panicked. He knew the right thing to do was to run back home and take the family South to Abyei town, but he also knew that he might get killed long before then.

"*Shit*," he swore but remained hidden in the bushes.

The cries continued until the sun had gone down. Kuol remained in the bushes, shedding tears despite himself.

At night, when the Messirya had retreated on their own account, Kuol went back home, knowing in his mind what would see there. His fore knowledge did not make the sight less disgusting. Bodies of men, women and children were heaped in the streets of Noong, and some had their arms and limbs severed. There were rumors the Messirya were going to use the severed parts to beat their drums as a sign of victory. Then the wails of surviving woman and children filled the air. Dogs barked in melancholia. Noong and the entire Ngok people were bleeding, physically and innwardly. The men promissed revenge.

Kuol watched the assembly that took place in Noong the following day. The nine chiefdoms were represented and with one objective: To put some pride back on the name of Ngok people and the Dinka people at large.

One man had stood up to talk, the first encounter Kuol had with the man who later became his Captain, Bagat Aguek. Kuol didn't remember what his soon to be Captain said, but the height and athletic build of the man had filled him with confidence.

Dozens of Ngok men matched northwards the following day,

though Kuol was not one of them. He heard later that the Messirya had been decisively defeated.

That defeat didn't hold the Messirya down for long, nor did it demoralize them. Two weeks later they were back, and on a bigger offensive with the strength of the Sudan Armed Forces behind them. Kuol and others in Noong had run southwards to Abyei town. The Messirya continued pushing their offensive. Bagat was there, mobilizing men to go to Bilpam and join the newly formed Sudan People's Liberation Movement and Army. Kuol had not planned to join but there was no choice anymore. A Jieng man did not choose to cower where he had a way of fighting back.

That was how Kuol had found himself fording the Kiir river one evening in May, as just one of Bagat's thousand men taking the journey to Bilpam.

* * *

"The Captain! Save the Captain!" A distant cry erupted.

Captain Kuol could hear it, but it was far. *Fantastic*, the call meant they were leaving the Messirya behind them. *The Captain was safe*.

He stepped on the wood and began to row while his Captain stood akimbo on the wooden raft, thinking like the strategist he was. Captain Bagat, ever gentle and down to earth, told Kuol to sit and let him row them instead.

Someone hit the wooden raft to make a gunshot sound. Tired, Kuol lay facedown on the raft. Water splashed on his face, and he moved to sit upright.

He awoke with a start, the thick forest staring back at him. He was seated in mud and had been dreaming. He, Captain Kuol, nicknamed the dogman for his watchfulness had slept off on duty.

"Cover the Captain!" Someone screamed. It was his nephew, Alor Biong. *Shit*, the Messirya had followed them this far. He had underestimated them.

He reached for his gun on the side only to find that it wasn't there. The Kalashnikov riffles screamed in the trees nearby, mixed with the distinct sound of a Patchett submachine gun.

Captain Kuol saw his gun a few yards away from him and dove for it.

An enemy combatant stepped out from behind a tree and shot. It hit him on the chest, and he knew no more.

Chapter 13

Sergeant Rou leaned against a tree, holding his gun, and took a deep breath.

Now!

He stepped out from behind a tree, just in time to see a Messirya take an aim at the Captain. The sergeant pulled the trigger without even thinking. It hit the the Messirya in the chest. *Take that you bastard!* The Messirya fell but somebody else fell with him.

"No!" Sergeant Rou screamed and ran out of his hidding place, shooting and shouting. The sound of gunshots could not stop him, he had eyes for only one, Captain Kuol.

Alor's heart sunk as he saw the Captain fall. He had failed to protect his uncle. The gun battle was intense and Alor couldnt't reach the Captain without getting himself killed. He shot, trying to clear the way. He watched as Sergeant Rou pulled his foolish stunt again. The man was practically running through a hail of bullets to reach the Captain. He kept running and shooting without even trying to take cover.

"Cover the Sergeant," Alor screamed but the armed members

did not need to be told. Only Sergeant Rou could take them to Bilpam, or they would be stuck in the forest and become prey.

Sergeant Rou's stunt seemed to be working. The Messirya reatreted.

Sergeant Rou ran on. He reached the Captain. He shook him but Captain Kuol did not stir. He just remained still. He looked to be in a deep slumber but there was blood on the side of his abdomen. The sergeant slung his gun on the shoulder and carried his Captain, praying silently in his heart that the sun of the bandits of Kiirkou had not set. Sergeant Rou did not find his voice to speak. He knew he was in commmand now, but he could not take over his duty, he was weak in body and mind.

"Take positions around the Captain and the sergeant!" Alor had taken command. *Brave young lad*, Sergeant Rou thought.

Sergeant Rou lay the Captain on the grass under a tree and began to attend to him. He cleaned the wound with a piece of cloth, but when the cloth was removed the blood began to ooze out. The sergeant's bone mending abilities were useless here, but he tried anyway. Massaging the side of the wound, trying to locate a broken bone. All the while, the Captain remained unconscious.

Alor Biong watched the Sergeant work from his sentry position as he and the others stood guard over the Captain. Alor had not decided about what to make of this man, Sergeant Rou. He had run through a hail of bullets and come out unscathed, not once but twice. The magazines on his waist were always ripped. *Maybe he has a magnet in his magazine porch, or the man has gotten a potent talisman from Damazin,* Alor found himself thinking.

Captain Kuol coughed from where he lay. Blood spurtered from his mouth. He tried to talk but the sound could not be heard. The Sergeant went on his knees and brought his ears closer to the Captain's mouth

"Take…. Ab…" Sergeant Rou looked puzzled. Alor came over.

"What is he saying Segeant?" Alor asked

"I can make neither head nor tail of what he said. Come. Hear it yourself."

Alor came down on his knees and listened, his ear close to the Captain's mouth.

"He sticks to the original plan, Sergeant. Abiemnom should be our destination."

"He should recover first, otherwise taking him to Abiemnom is going to be a challenge, but if the Captain says so, off to Abiemnom we go then."

The boys made a stretcher with spare clothes and logs and lay the Captain on it.

The March then began.

By the end of the first night, the bandits of Kiirkou were still surrounded by impenetrable forests with no end yet in sight. They took rest as night fell. The Captain wasn't any better, but he had atleast began to speak haltingly and yet the things he said did not make sense to Alor or the Sergeant. He looked like he was deep in a dream.

* * *

Kuol Deng ran through the forest with his Captain, Bagat Aguek. They were somewhere near the border of the Upper Nile and Unity states, and the Sudan Armed Forces were patrolling the area. Captain Bagat and his thousand Ngok men had to be stealthy or be killed.

They ran by night and hid by day. As a young man, Kuol Dengstuck around Captain Bagat because the few guns that the thousand possessed were concentrated around him.

Ten days of crossing the border and going deeeply into the Shilluk areas devasted the thousand, who lost some of their members. One day, the Captain's crew were met by armed Southerners, about two thousand strong. The crew were surrounded and outnumbered.

"Where are you headed brothers," The leader of the armed Southerners asked.

Captain Bagat did not take a second to answer

"To join John Garang's SPLA." He said, sure that he had met members of the movement.

"Why not the Anyanay II?" The leader said, and turned his back to the Captain, but Captain Bagat did not answer. The leader walked behind the wall created around the Ngok men by his men.

"KIll them!" He said, and the Kalashnikov rifles spat fire. The wall of Ngok men around Captain Bagat collapsed. Kuol Deng screamed.

***

"Captain!" Sergeant Rou exclaimed.

The Captain was sitting upright on the stretcher, screaming at the top of his voice, while blood gushed from the wound on his abdomen. Sergeant Rou held him down fast until he regained his senses and kept quiet, laying down on the stretcher which was now a red mess of blood.

"Trap," the Captain kept saying in his half sleep. Sergeant Rou wanted to send for Alor, but the young lad already come running.

"They did not retreat, sergeant," Alor said, breathless, "they have been following us. The Captain's scream did not do much good because they can tell how far we are. I saw a sentry run back to report, and I couldn't get him because the undergrowrh was too thick and hard to see through."

***

Captain Kuol lay in the pool of blood. He could feel something sticky and warm on his back, but it was distant, as if his body belonged to someone else. He could see distant images of himself and Captain Bagat, plus a few survivors, running through the bushes and dodging their hunters. He was lagging, and Captain Bagat was leaving him behind, while the armed Southerners closed in. He tried to scream but he couldn't.

No. The men were getting closer to him each passing second.

No. He tried his best to run, but everthing about him was heavy. The men were near enough to him now, and one of them aimed, pulling the trigger.

"Nooo!" Captain Kuol screamed for the second time that day.

The crew looked alarmed and made a circle around their Captain, forgetting the Messirya threat. By the time they recovered, the damage had already been done. Kalashnikov rifles screamed all around them and the men panicked. Two of the crew fell within no time.

"Carry the Captain," Sergeant Rou shouted. Two of the crew shouldered the stretcher and headed in the direction that the Sergeant pointed. The rest of the crew tried to hold back the Messirya. They stood their ground and fired, but more and more Messirya seemed to come out from the woods.

To sergeant Rou, the possibility of being surrounded seemed imminent.

"Retreat!" he shouted to the boys as another of the crew fell. The remaining five ran helter skelter through the woods, a tactical retreat longer possible. They reached where the Captain had been put down.

"Carry the Captain you fools!" Sergeant Rou said but the men simply looked at the Captain who rose into a sitting position on the stretcher.

"Give me a gun, Sergeant. I'll cover your retreat. Remember, any armed person you meet within the borders of Sudan is an enemy unless proven otherwise."

"No such a thing Captain," said sergeant Rou, "we are taking you to Bilpam."

The Messirya kept closing in. Capatin Kuol glanced around and murmured,

"I feared as much."

He grabbed a gun from a nearby crew member and put the muzzle in his mouth, pulling the trigger.

"Nooo!" the entire crew shouted in unison.

The Messirya paused. Captain Kuol lay there, blood flowing from his mouth, a shaddow of his former self.

CHAPTER 14

Major General Gatluak Deng divided his men into ten groups and sent them into the bushes with orders to lure any Bilpam bound recruits into their camp. Things had not gone so well for the Anyanya II so far, but Gatluak had no doubt in his mind that they would grow bigger than the SPLA and eventually absorb them into their ranks.

The leadership had sent a message inviting the Anya II of Northern Bahrelghazel to join them, but it had now been two months and yet not a reply had come. General Gatluak prefered not to guess their reply, but he had known it. No matter how liberal a man is, he tends to bend towards his family and his tribe. The Anyanya II would appear in Bilpam to support their tribesmen.

General Gatluak had spent the late '70s with the Anyanya II battling the Sudanese army. Instead of thanking him and the other leaders of Anyanya II, the Southerners entered their camp in a large number, bringing with them an inexperienced Colonel with bogus ranks, calling him their leader. General Gatluak shook his head. There is no greater insult to an army man than appointing his junior to a position of superirity over him.

The soldiers lined up before him in their twenty groups, squads of twelve each. He moved around, inspecting their equipment. He took it in all, the dire state of the rifles they held. Some were covered with rust while others were pre-world war one muskets that caused more noise than harm to the enemy. He noted the nature of his men. Malnurished but capable of great acts of hero-ism. These men had dedicated their lives to the complete liberation of the marginalized people of the Southern Sudan.

"Listen men!" said General Gatluak, pacing before the the asssemply of twenty groups in green military camouflage, "if you meet groups of Southerners, ask them where they are headed. Let their answer decide their fate. Those whose answer is to join the SPLA, kill them. If their answer is to join the struggle, bring them to the camp."

The Soldiers marched away into the bushes in their groups, each taking a different direction. Two Sudan Armed force branded military tanks loitered around camp. Food and amunitions had arrived. The war of kinsmen was just beginning.

PART THREE

THE GATHERING OF THE STORM

Chapter 15

Bakhita Nyanut looked around. She kept looking for something new, something she had never seen before because this was Bilpam, the famed place. Nobody had ever told her what Bilpam was while she was in Aweil. All Nyanut knew was that people came to Bilpam to get their guns to fight the Arabs. Now that she was here, she wanted to see what was so extraordinary about Bilpam and what set it apart from other places.

All around were a myriad of grass thatched huts and tents with thousands of people moving about. Nyanut felt excited. She knew that somewhere in those huts and tents, people were devising a strategem for liberation of the marginalized people of the Sudan. She surveyed the huts and tents with renewed interest. General Doka shifted beside her, and she realised she wasn't alone.

The old General kept stroking his grey stricken beards and looking around suspiciously.

Nyanut liked the old General, because no sooner had the General become part of the crew, than captain Kon Lual began to keep his distance from her. For once in a long time, she felt herself.

The crew were led to the commanding officers in Bilpam by the sentries who had found them moving towards the base. The soldiers stopped suddenly outside a hut.

"Tell the commander in chief we have visitors," said the leader of the soldiers to the guards.

"The commander is busy and won't see anyone today," one of the guards replied.

"Uh Uhum," General Doka cleared his voice and Nyanut couldn't help but glance at him, "tell the Commander that General Yusif Doka has come to see him. "

"General Doka, the lion of the Immatong who survived ten ambushes and five bullets to the chest?" The guard asked, eyes wide.

General Doka bowed theatrically, and the guard rushed into the hut.

It did not take long for the commander to step out. He was a tall middle-aged man with a sizeable belly and a bald head. It took Nyanut some time to connect stories she had heard to understand what was happening. Here was the man, the legend and the hope of Sudan's oppressed people, Dr. John Garang De Mabior.

He greeted General Doka like the old comrade he was, as they had fought together before the Addis Ababa agreement. He was not the man she had imagined he would be, he was too soft. She had imagined a tough authoritative man to whom all bowed.

* * *

After Dr. John had re-entered the hut with General Doka, the rest in the company were shown to little huts to sleep. Some were asked to sleep in the open, under trees where there were dry spots. The entire camp was flooded from the rain.

Bakhita Nyanut and Old man were given the same hut to share with two other women. The beds were made of logs so high they almost reached the ceiling. The hut was flooded, with water that reached to the knees. Nyanut saw the two other women in the room washing their faces in it. Disgusting.

"What difference does it make?" Said one of them as if in answer to Nyianut's unasked question.

Nyanut glanced at Aker Deng aka Old man who did not seem disheartened at the very least. She lay on the bed and had already striked up a conversation with the two other women in the room.

"They are out to starve the populations down in Bahr el ghazal. While in Equatoria, they are turning the populations against the SPLA." Aker Deng was saying.

"We have heard as much," said one of the women, "but worse things are happening in the Upper Nile state and the adjacent areas. You were lucky to have taken the longer, safer route."

"How is that?" asked Old Nan.

"All those found to be coming to join SPLA are killed by Anyanya II before they can make it here."

Aker Deng sat bolt upright on the bed and hung her head.

"Why would a Southerner do that to another Southerner?" she asked.

"No matter how close people are, the rot sets in as soon as the question of leadership arises. Ambition knows no relations."

Nyanut and listened quietly. What Aker and the other woman were saying brought back bitter memories of Aweil, and how Garang's body was hauled onto a truck. She longed to get hold of a gun because no matter how many enemies were from within, she had promised herself long time ago that master Abdallah would die by her hand alone, God willing. Nyanut fell asleep, while Aker and the other woman talked on.

Fatigue overwhelmed her. She dreamed of Makom village before the Rhezigat had wrecked havoc on it.

* * *

Bol lay under a tree, on a little sack, placed on a dry spot. He knew in his heart that he had no regrets about making the journey to Bilpam but that didn't stop him from thinking of Aweil. There, he had had a roof over his head and a blanket to warm himself. In Bilpam, he was at the mercy of the god of weather.

So far, it was not raining, but he could hear the rumble of thunder in the sky. If it rained, he didn't know what he and his companions would do. They had just arrived and had had no time to put up a little shelter for themselves.

The thunder rumbled again. No sleep for us today then, he thought. He looked at his companions who looked thoughtful themselves. It began to drizzle with little scattered drops, then it began to rain fully. It was a hailstorm. The soldiers collected all the firearms and took them to the armoury.

Bol and his companions huddled together near the trunk of a tree. The hail struck painfully. It tore their clothes, the ones that they had worn continuously for months neither changing nor washing. None of them spoke. They faced the adverse weather in silence. Each praying to his god that lightning didn't strike them. It was not the reception they had expected, at least not the one Bol had expected.

Dawn found them lying helter shelter under the tree, some in pools of water sleeping soundly. The lucky ones like Bol had found drier spots and lay there to sleep. The rain had stopped a few hours before dawn.

"Piiip! Piiiiiip!"

The Kapoeta crew woke up to long whistle blasts. Those who had been soldiers realised that it was parade time but those who had never been in a barracks, like Bol, could make neither head nor tail of it. He turned and began to sleep, but lieutenant Kwaje wouldn't let him. He kicked him gently and Bol sat up, still sleepy.

"Parade time! " the lieutenant shouted

Bol understood and ran to join his colleagues.

* * *

The parade was organised in long lines. There were lines of experienced soldiers, lines of men who had never been soldiers, lines of women, and lines of young boys known as the red army. In front of the assembly stood the chief of staff. Bol did not get most of what he said, but he liked the songs because most of the speech was punctuated by songs from the army's musicians.

Chapter 16

Nyanut stood attention, the way she saw other girls and women standing. Beside her, Aker Deng aka old man stood erect, a posture Nyanut admired but couldn't emulate. The fatigue from the months long journey on foot had now gone into her bones especially after the previous night's rest. She thought she would fall over, but she didn't. She was stronger than she gave herself credit for.

The Captains handled the four groups, recording names. All the people in the parade were new arrivals to Bilpam, but Nyanut didn't know that. The Captain handling the women and girls reached Nyanut.

"What's your name?"

"My name is Bakhita Nyanut Garang Nyan Paduil."

The Captain laughed. "I'm not here to court you," he said, "though that might come later, who knows." He jotted down her name and continued with his task. Next in line was Aker Deng aka old man. "Your name?"

"Aker Deng" She replied, and the Captain almost jumped. She

99

had a voice he associated with men and not with women. The Captain raised his eyebrows but did not say anything. He moved on to the next in line. Soon, the exercise was over, and the next phase began.

* * *

"Bakhita Nyanut-Rhino." The Captain read and Nyanut glanced around, puzzled.

"Amou Bak- Cobra, " the Captain continued, "Aker Deng - Rhino, "

Nyanut glanced at Aker Deng, but she was calm, like she understood what was going on.

"Achol Akot- Scorpion."

Nyanut tugged at the eldery woman's sleeve, "What's going on?" she asked. "Weren't you informed?" asked Old Nan.

"No," Nyanut shook her head.

"We came late, but still early enough to be incorporated into the battalions of the Koryom division. You and I are in Rhino Batallion."

Nyanut did not understand what a battalion meant. She had never known much about the army because she had never been near the army, but she did not ask Aker. Nyanut felt her intestines turn. She was going to be separated from her new family again. She did not weep. Aker Deng was with her, and that was reassuring. Perhaps Bol, General Doka or even Captain Kon Lual would be in Rhino battalion too.

* * *

"Bol Deng- Rhino" The Captain read. Bol took a moment to

realize it was his name being called. It was uncanny to be called a name he hadn't used in years. When he had travelled through all the counties of Aweil over the years and even moved through most of Southern Sudan on his way to Bilpam, his name had been Bol. Just Bol. No second name. He hated his second name, and avoided it like a plague whenever possible, because he hated the man who owned it. That was not possible today because the Captain demanded to know his feather's name and he had not been quick enough to think of a fake one.

Rhino battalion. Bol was overjoyed. He had done his homework and knew that Rhino battalion would be heading to Bahr el ghazal region. He breathed in deeply and exhaled, because he would avenge Garang and in the process, might have a chance to kick master Abdallah. He decided he would only return to Pan Apuoth once he had attained a certain rank in the army specifically a rank high enough to grant him an enormous escort. He could already see and enjoy the look on Dengdit's face as his useless son turned up with an escort of a dozen men. He smiled again at the thought.

"Dut Kuan -Zindia," the Captain read on.

The Captain's voice woke Bol from his daydream.

"Shit!" He realized; he hadn't even started training yet.

* * *

General Yusif Doka sat at a table and read through an enormous list of potential Rhino battalion soldiers. Potential, because the bulk of them were absolute civilians who had never carried a gun let alone fire it. They were supposed to be battle ready in a month. General Doka oversaw operations and had to report to the overall commander of the battalion. It was as if he had gone back in time, fifteen years, when he had handled most Anyanya operations in Equatoria region.

He knew what would come next.

It was all like a movie scene in real life, as unreal as it was real. There would be killing and killing and then there would be an agreement to share power. He pulled out maps of Bahrelghazel from under the table and studied them for the uptenth time.

He had tried to tell Dr John that he knew Equatoria like the back of his palm, but the same wouldn't be said of Bahr el ghazel, though the man would have none of it. Back in Anyanya I, the good colonel had been just one of the many Anyanya soldiers and he, Doka had been one of the important leaders. Now the tables had turned, and the former subordinate had become the superior. The old General understood well how things change but it still baffled him why the colonel wouldn't use him where he would serve best. He looked at the names, and for a moment allowed himself to feel sorry for the recruits, young men and women who had convinced themselves that they were fighting for freedom.

These young people would wake up after so much fighting, the survivors that is, only to realize that an agreement that did not benefit them had been signed. General Doka stared at the maps and hoped he was wrong about the SPLA; he hoped its leaders were not the same as the Anyanya leaders.

He unfolded the maps and sat back in his chair. He had never been to most parts of Bahrelghazal region, but he knew a few places by name from his previous stint as a General. Here was Yirol, Rumbek, Tonj, all with a significant military presence, before you made it to Wau. Doka doubted they would make it as far as Aweil because that would require a lot of payment in blood, and SPLA could not afford that.

He refolded the maps and placed them in a drawer. He had to

see the commander of his battalion; a Lieutenant Colonel Martin Maku, Makil… he could not even remember his commander's name. He hated working under people, but then, nobody liked being a subordinate, especially not in the army.

* * *

Lieutenant Kwaje did not like what he saw and especially did not like how he was being treated. He was a man with more than fifteen years of military service under his belt, five of those had been spent in combat against the Sudan Armed Forces and a further five had been spent surpressing uprisings. With a wealth of combat experience, he had thought that he would have a claim to leadership in the SPLA but the bastards in charge had other ideas. He, lieutenant Kwaje, with all his experience, was now to serve under some green youth whose only qualification was a diploma from a fancy military college in Cuba.

He would serve anyway, he promised himself, and he would make them see the wonders of having experience. He left to look for Doka whom he was sure was no longer a general by now but instead had some modest rank.

Chapter 17

The four of them looked grim and exhausted, so far, the lowest number of any arrivals into Bilpam. They looked at each other and smiled, they had just escaped something akin to hell. They looked at other new arrivals who showed pity for the four, but the four smiled. They had mourned enough colleagues along the way and tears no longer meant anything. They had tasted battle and were now battle hardened. They clutched their guns closely.

Alor Biong was positive he would never forget Nasir and Akobo. He had been positive he would die every moment he spent between those two towns, yet just when he was about to give up, sergeant Rou was always there pulling off his stunt, the bullets richocheting off the magazines on his hips. Alor didn't care whether it was a magnet on the man's hip or one of those talismans from Damazin, he was just happy to be alive.

Men fell around them like flies, some were members of the bandits of Kiirkou, others were those who joined them along the way. He knew he would have nightmares for the rest of his life but so long as he was alive, he was ok with the nightmares. He was beginning to hate the Southern traitors more than the Arab regime.

The four grim bandits were a spectacle at the camp for a few days, even after their guns had been taken from them, but they faded into the background as they recovered their strength and became just another group of civilians come to join the popular struggle.

"Pip piiiiip!" The whistle blew. Three days since their arrival and the former bandits had never been called to the parade because their physical condition was bad.

Today however, they were to attend with the newest arrivals and get assigned to a battalion each.

"Alor Biong- Rhino," The Captain in charge read

Alor shifted and paid attenion. He prayed in his heart for Sergeant Rou to be in the same battalion with him.

"Koang Chuol- Lion"

"Ronyo Ajak- Hippo"

"John Lomodong - Elephant"

Alor shifted to one foot from where he stood and continued listening. This was taking too long. He held his breath and glanced at sergeant Rou while the Captain shuffled the papers in his hand.

"Rou Monyluak- Rhino"

Alor breathed a sigh of relief; Sergeant Rou was coming to Bahrelghazal with him. He knew that the rank of sergeant had disappeared since it was only bestowed upon him when he was a bandit, but nevertheless to Alor he would always be the sergeant. His sergeant.

* * *

"Rou Monyluak" sounded hollow to the man who owned the name because he had grown accustomed to the title of Sergeant.

When the Captain read the name without the title it took him a few seconds to realize he was called. He glanced at Alor. He was going to Bahrelghazal with the young boy, and Rou was happy because it gave him the opportunity to be close to Alor. He looked around and saw that the two other remnants of the bandits of Kiirkou were staring at him, undoubtedly, they wanted to be in the same battalion as him. He wanted to tell them that he really didn't know what he did whenever the battle frenzy overcame him, that they should be more afraid of him than adore him. Supposing during the frenzy he ended up shooting them instead of the enemy?

He wouldn't even begin to talk about it, and nobody had asked him, at least not yet. They instead looked at him with reverence like a god and he let them.

When the parade ended, he and Alor were confirmed to be in Rhino battalion. The other two bandits were in Lion and Hippo, and they were about to lodge a complaint, but the sergeant managed to talk them out of it. He assured them that such a complaint would land them in trouble for insubordination even before their military careers had begun and after talking, the two saw the wisdom of his argument.

Rou Monyluak pulled Alor aside.

"Listen," he began

"Yes, sergeant?" Alor said.

"Don't call me that."

"Sorry. It's just out of habit. This will take some time."

"Ok listen, your uncle, Captain Kuol left us abruptly, but I'm sure he would want us to meet Captain Bagat and inform him about his activities before he died. Bilpam is a big place as you can see. Captain Bagat could be in this hut," he said, pointing to a nearby hut "Or the one over there."

Alor listened but did not interrupt. The mention of his uncle brought back the emotions he had burried. Alor felt guilty, he hadn't even been able to bury his uncle. He didn't know what he would tell his father if they ever met again.

"Let's begin the search then," Alor said and at that moment, he began praying that they did not find Captain Bagat. He dreaded the man's reaction should he be told that his friend was dead and rotting somewhere in the forests of Abiemnom.

They asked some soldiers for Captain Bagat but were told there were at least five Captains of that name in Bilpam.

"Did they remember his father's name?" the soldiers asked.

They did not and Captain Kuol had never talked about Captain Bagat's second name.

They made rounds through the camp in their search but to no avail. By the end they were tired to the bone and staggering back to their sleeping quarters, when it hit Alor.

Yes, he knew the man's second name. His uncle had told him once but his memory, his once sharp memory was beginning to fail him somehow. He stopped.

"Sergeant. I mean Uncle Rou," Alor said.

"What is it?" Rou asked, confused.

"I think I remember Captain Bagat's second name."

"Come on! how would you ever remember what you have never known?"

"I heard it from my late uncle once. The name is Aguek, Captain Bagat Aguek."

The two walked back to ask the soldiers and sure enough there was a Captain Bagat Aguek, but he was out of camp on a mission, and both knew enough about the army rules not to ask what sort. They turned back but not before locating the Captain's quarters.

It was already evening when they reached their side of the

camp. They passed by the mess where they and other new recruits scrambled for food; posho and peas.

They all but fought for it. Some of the recruits had been there long enough to learn the subtle art of not feeling the heat of the posho, hence an advantage over the newly arrived. By the time they finished, which was within seconds, Alor's stomach was as empty as he had gone to the mess with it. He and uncle Rou gulped down some water, and walked to their shelter where they threw themselves on a straw bed and closed their eyes, each knowing the other was awake, but not bothering to talk. They had anticipated a battle with the Arabs but not the battle with hunger.

* * *

There were two whistle blasts, and the two men were already out of the hut. It was parade time, and they were among the first ones on the parade grounds. The soldiers watched them with awe because it was unusual for untrained civilians to be so punctual. Hell, even trained soldiers found it hard to be punctual at times. It was seven o'clock in the morning and the officer on duty blew the whistle for the fifth time. Two loud long blasts and the new recruits and soldiers streamed onto the parade grounds. When the parade was finally set, Alor noticed that they weren't as many as there had been in previous parades.

One of the officers in charge unfurled a flag infront of the parade with a black Rhino on a green background. Under the picture of the Rhino was written in block capital letters, 'RHINO BATTALION'. He read it with ease. His little education had given him that much.

Alor instinctively looked around to see the people that would be making it to Bahr el Ghazal with him, just a few hundred people in his estimates, all from various tribes. The group was divided into two, with a Captain handling each.

The two Captains began assigning the Rhino battalion soldiers and the new recruits into the various combat units of the batallion. Alor Biong and his former sergeant were meant to be together, as they found themselves in the same unit, yet again under the new arrangement. Alor was distracted, he had eyes only for another young member of the batallion who was to be a member of their new unit. He smiled shyly.

"Beautiful, isn't she?" Rou whispered close to his ears and Alor jumped. The older man smiled wickedly.

Chapter 18

Did he just smile at me? It had been years since anyone smiled at her, at least in a well meaning way. What she had just seen was a genuine smile, the kind of smile she last received in Makom some three years ago.

Nyanut dismissed it and maybe she had only imagined it. No boy would fall for her again, she was used, broken by older people until she no longer looked her age. The last she had looked at herself in a mirror, she had barely recognized the person that stared back. In any case I am in the same unit with the boy, she told herself and I will find out soon if I was daydreaming or not.

She glanced around at her new family, the combat unit. Almost everybody from her Kapoeta crew were in the unit, except for lieutenant Kwaje. Aker Deng aka old man was there, Bol was there, Dut was there. Even captain Kon Lual was there, but Nyanut wasn't afraid of him because General Doka was a higher-ranking officer.

The boy who smiled at her stood talking to an older man. Nyanut stole a glance at him. Just one glance and she remembered her mum telling her not to glance at boys. She hadn't understood back then but she understood now.

She would not let the boy know she was smitten. A woman was to be approached and a man loved a woman more if he struggled to get her. Nyanut would play hardball.

As soon as everyone had been assigned a unit, the parade resumed but it had taken a new shape. There were now four combat units, and each stood distinctly from the other. The commander of the battalion, lieutenant colonel Martin stood in front of the parade flanked on either side by General Doka, who was no longer a General but retained the name out of respect for his heroics and the battalion chief of military intelligence.

The commander began to address the parade. He cleared his voice and began,

"Young men and women, I greet you all with as much respect as possible. You deserve it. You deserve it, because all of you who stand before me have answered a noble call to arms. A call to fight for our freedom. A call to reclaim that which was snatched from us at the Juba conference." He paused as if to let his listeners digest what he had just communicated while he wiped his forehead with a hankerchief.

"Doubtless, many of you have witnessed grave atrocities on your way here, if not experienced them. North in Aweil, the scorched earth policy is in full swing and old people, women and children are starving even at this very moment. In Wau not long ago, they stormed a wedding, killing civilians who had in no way wronged them, their only crime being that they were happy. According to them, the southerner is to live and die sad. They hate it when you and I are happy. Who is the 'they' I refer to?" The General posed the question to the gathering before him without really expecting them to give him an answer.

"It's not the northerners," He continued. "The people of Nuba mountains are as oppressed as us, the Darfur people are just as oppressed. Who oppresses us then? The Arabs!" he followed that with a jab into the air with the small club he held in his hand.

"Who killed Father Saturnino Lohure?"

"The Arabs!" A young man in one of the combat units shouted.

The General took note and continued,

"Who ambushed William Deng Nhial in the forests between Rumbek and Tonj and killed him?"

"The Arabs!" Voices shouted in unison, taking an example from the first man/

"Who knowingly sent colonel Manuel Abur to his death?"

"The Arabs!" the whole parade intoned.

"For decades they have enslaved most of our kin or sold them into slavery."

"The Arabs!"

"They rape our mothers and sisters at will."

"The Arabs!"

"They deliberately supported the kokora to divide and rule us!"

"The Arabs!"

"They raped the Addis Ababa agreement!"

"The Arabs!"

Lieutenant colonel Martin wiped his forehead with a hankerchief again. The sun was now up, and it shone brightly on Bilpam. His green uniform looked startlingly striking under the rays of the early morning sunshine. The red rank collar patches on his neck took on the look of a glowing splint. The recruits stood, outraged and ready to tear any Arab into pieces should any surface.

"Ladies and gentlemen, this by no means will be the first time we are fighting the Arabs. We have done so before but this time we will not settle for any micky mouse agreement. We are fighting for change. We are fighting for a new Sudan. We are Rhino battalion of Koryom division, and we will descend onto Bahr el Ghazal like the locusts after which we have been named. We will pierce them and push them with the brute strength of a Rhino. We will push them north, to Egypt where they belong. To do that effectively, all of you who have never been soldiers will undergo training starting from tomorrow."

The lieutenant colonel stopped and the officer in charge took the platform.

"Katiba rhino Oyee!" he said at the top of his voice

"Oyee!" The parade erupted like thunder.

"Katiba rhino oyee!"

"Oyee!"

* * *

General Yusif Doka, who was now just a Major yet still called a General, stood beside the commander and watched the young man whose lone voice had turned the commander's otherwise boring speech into a heartwarming one. He wondered whether the boy knew that he had saved the commander's day and that if an agreement was crafted for power sharing, that the Generals would accept it.

Indeed, only the good doctor seemed to have different ideas from his Anyanya predecessors, the rest of the Generals and politicians were strikingly Anyanyasque in ideology and they seemed about just ready to accept any deal in a year or two. Yusif Doka was sure they would sign any agreement without reading it and if they happened to read it, they would misunderstand like their Anyanya brothers had in 1972.

The boy has potential, Yusif Doka decided and it did not matter if the boy knew or did not know. He had courage and that was

just about enough for the army, this army at least. He would seek
the boy out later.

* * *

"I hate surprises, you know," Rou Monyluak said when the two
were inside their little hut and lying on the straw bed, "you should
let me in on your plans more often. Here you were, interrupting
a commander's speech."

"That wasn't really planned, I stood there and suddenly, I was
inspired. I don't know how to explain it to you, I just felt it was
the right thing to say." Alor said.

Rou shook his head. "I hope this is the last one because this is
the army. Remember never to look or act too clever because the
instructors hate smart ass recruits. They try to break them. Trust
me, you wouldn't want to be on the wrong side of an instructor."

"How would you know all that. You have never been in the
army."

Rou smiled. "I just know," he said cheerfully but he wasn't
cheerful. His mind had raced back in time, to a time he had never
wanted to remember, a time he was ashamed of.

* * *

It came back vividly. His friends had told him to stay away from
Fatima but Rou, just like many adolescents wouldn't listen, he
wanted her, and she wanted him. To the young Rou, that was all
that mattered. It was a free world, and he could choose who to
love provided they loved him back.

Rou never learned who tipped off Fatima's father because no
matter how confident his adolescence had made him; Rou had
had the decency to at least keep his love with Fatima a secret.

It was a surprise when soldiers broke into their family house in Omdurman in 1962, caned everyone they could lay hands on, beating Rou unconscious. When he came to, Rou found himself in a dark room. It took him time to recollect what had happened before he blacked out.

"Father, let me kill him," A voice said from what Rou assumed was the door, because he could see faint light streaming into the room from that end. He tried to stand up but found he was chained to the floor. His whole body screamed in pain. He wondered how long he had been unconscious.

"No, Omar, we have disciplined him enough, take him to the barracks. We don't want Jenge blood on our hands." A second, elderly voice said, "he will die fighting his Jenge brethren, the Anyanya."

The room opened and a young man about five years older than Rou walked in dangling keys in his hands. Rou could only see his silhouette against the faint light from the open door.

"Stupid Jenge bastard," he spat on his prisoner and kicked his head. Rou just had enough time to identify what had connected with his head, a heavy military boot, before blacking out again.

In different ways, Rou Monuak has always thought that he never really came to again after Omar's kick on his head. He joined the army, forced to join rather, and had escaped from it years later to join the bandits of Kirrkou. Yet everything always seemed like a bad dream.

CHAPTER 19

"Op! Op!" The recruits moaned as the heavy logs weighed them down. Rows upon rows of ten men were spread on the field, each row with a heavy log of wood over their shoulders, crouching and standing in a rhythm. A week ago, one of them would have fallen and fainted with exhaustion, but not anymore. They were stronger, and it showed. Sweat dripped from naked chests. Not that the recruits cared, they had to crouch fifty times with the log over their shoulders.

Major Yusif Doka, who was the instructor, fished a box of super matches out of his pocket and selected a piece. He lit it and puffed.

"Rest!" Maj. Doka commanded, smoke escaping from his nostrils. The squad leaders repeated the order throughout and the recruits happily tossed the logs aside and stretched, each of them having found out that trying to rest on those short breaks didn't make them ready for the next drill exercise, it only weakened them.

"Fall in!" Maj. Yusif Doka said abruptly, and the entire battalion rushed to their feet and stood in a formation at the position of attention.

"Parade rest!"

The recruits spread their feet in silence with arms clasped behind their backs. Maj. Yusif Doka moved from combat unit to combat unit, giving out penalties at will.

"You!" he said to one recruit who stood a bit clumsily.

"Yes, sir!"

Major Doka realized that it was the young boy who had previously saved the commander's day, and the boy's feet were shaking from crouching.

"Fifty squats for you in two minutes. Your time starts now!" The boy started immediately, looking as though he might faint on the spot.

Many were immersed in water and made to crawl on their knees and elbows. Major Doka smiled. Character as an important virtue of a soldier can only be developed by passing recruits through difficult training, some of which take the shape torture. Every recruit would pass through that before they graduated.

*　*　*

Alor Biong went over it again and again in his head:

Alpha Bravo and Charlie Delta's feet Echo as they do a Foxtrot at Golf Hotel India with Juliet and Kilo Lima. Mike November and Oscar Papa are in Quebec dreaming of a Sierra while Tango as a Uniform Victor drunk Whiskey and did an X-ray on the weird Yankee Zulu.

He was finding it hard to learn the NATO phonetic Alphabet and had devised a way to memorize it, no matter how senseless the two sentences he had come up with sounded. He lay on his straw bed and chanted the sentences of memorization softly to himself.

His body was sore and aching. When he first came to Bilpam,

he had thought that he had already gone through enough training with the bandits of Kiirkou and wouldn't need more. He saw that he had been very mistaken, because there was more to being a soldier than just shooting guns and running around. You needed to be very fit, and not just physically but mentally as well.

Alor saw that the General over worked people, but he realized that everyone had to go through this tedious process to become a soldier, and there was no backing out. What would one do if one backed out? Cook for the 'men' who went on to become soldiers?

Alor felt that that sort of humiliation would kill him, but the intense training wouldn't.

Someone stagered into the hut. It was Rou Monyluak. Alor watched him from the bed where he lay. Rou was breathing heavily, and bleeding from his elbows and knees.

"What happened to you?" Alor asked, alarmed.

"They made me fly." Rou said and fell to the ground like a sack of flour. Alor carried him to the bed and started to clean his wounds.

Being made to fly was a very bad, very dangerous thing. Four soldiers held the victim's two hands, and the other two dealt with the legs. They would suspend the victim in midair like an airplane and drop him to the ground from a very great height. Many broke their ribs in that manner, and it was a very inhumane punishment, but the military police have loved inhumane ways since time immemorial.

Rou slept badly that night and when he woke up the following day, he found that his body was all sore, but he stretched anyway. He had been a soldier once and had experienced worse injuries than the ones he had now. There was a whistle blast, and Rou woke Alor.

* * *

Rou Monyluak held the practice gun while they showed him where he was supposed to hit. The target was a piece of red cloth, with a small black drawing on it. Everyone had to hit the black spot and so far, many had tried and missed. Rou rested the gun chamber on his chest and aimed. Applause erupted among the recruits. He had hit the bull's eye. They gave him another, thinking he had hit it by mistake, but he hit bull's eye again.

General Doka who was watching the practice noted down something in his small notebook.

They saw how Rou did with artillery guns, but he wasn't so good at it. The young Bol Deng seemed to have a talent for artillery pieces.

The following day, the graduation parade was called, and promotions were given to the exceptional trainees.

"Awan Bol," the Captain assigned to read the promotions read, "hereafter promoted to first lieutenant." Awan walked in front and was decorated by Generals Martin and Doka.

"Bol Deng. Hereafter promoted to 2nd lieutenant."

Rou Monyluak was promoted to his previous bandit rank of Sergeant.

PART FOUR

A TIME
OF RECKONING

CHAPTER 20

The locusts entered Sudan through Nasr town; hell bent on settling scores that dated back to time immemorial. They came in a destructive wave and wherever they passed, the countryside was left silent, save for a few scattered jubilations of the liberated who dared not applaud fully lest the oppressors returned and avenged their dead. They were the locusts of the Sudan People's Liberation Army and unlike their insect counterparts they left the countryside green. Green, but littered with the blood of the Sudan Armed Forces and their allied militias.

* * *

"Blue, this is Green. Can you read? One- Two- Three- Four... this is Green." A voice came from a CB radio General Doka held.

"Go ahead Green, I've got you, " General Doka said. "This is Blue"

"Urgent report. Enemy warship sighted along the Nile, grid coordinates Echo-Foxtrot-Seven-Niner-Two-Three-six. Estimated distance, 10 kilometers from our position. Warship appears to be hostile and has heavy armaments. Requesting immediate instructions, over."

"Copy, Green. Your swift report is appreciated. Maintain visual observation without compromising your position. Deploy squad into cover and maintain radio silence. Amara is en route to reinforce your position. Gather intel on enemy movements, including troop activity and potential intentions. Await Amara's rendezvous and await further directives. Do not engage unless provoked. Acknowledge, over."

"Roger that, Blue. Squad is in concealment, maintaining visual observation on warship's activities. Radio silence enforced. We'll gather comprehensive intel on troop movements promptly. Amara's support eagerly awaited. Will engage only if threatened, over."

"Green, your dedication to the mission acknowledged. Amara will establish communication upon arrival. Transmit intel on enemy movements at regular intervals once the communication is re-established. Maintain situational awareness. Out."

General Doka put down the radio and sighed. The adventure was beginning sooner than he had expected. The clouds above wept and rain poured in thick and chilly drops. Their hide out did not include shelters, and General Doka's athritis had started to respond to the cold. He could feel it in both his feet and hands, and it felt as if something was gnawing his bones.

The vessel slid along the Nile. Alor watched it from where he hid, reminded of snakes that slid on the surface of the Nyamora back in Abyei. The vessel made its way through the Nile, effortlessly and Alor was mesmerized despite the danger it posed. He had never seen or heard of it.

He watched it come, like something out of an American movie, where an American warship slides along a river in the jungles of

Vietnam while birds twittter gleefully in the background. The only addition here, was the crickets chirping too. All human sounds were as if extinct for a moment, which to Alor seemed like hours. As the warship drew closer, Alor could see men on the deck looking relaxed. General Doka had said that the army had not expected the rebels to move against them too soon and Alor believed him now.

The men who sat on deck the warship wore the colours of the Sudanese navy, white with blue shoulder pads. The warship slid along, making ripples and bubbles on the water behind it. Alor held his breath from where he hid and cocked his gun.

He was to fire three warning shots towards the warship, on the count of three from Lieutenant Bol, who stood next to him. The Lieutenant wasn't much older than Alor.

He lifted his hand up, rolled into a fist. One! He indicated by raising a finger and paused, two! He added another finger. Alor kept watching him all the while wondering what would happen when he fired those warning shots towards the warship, would it shoot? He didn't have to wonder much because Lieutenant Bol suddenly added another finger and Alor's hands acted by reflex. Before he could even think about it, he felt the gun tremble in his hand.

Three bullets landed one after another just a few yards short of the warship which stopped abruptly. Birds flew from trees in unison, confused. Somewhere on the opposite bank, Alor saw the black, red and green of the Sudan People's Liberation army emerge from the thickets as the wind blew.

* * *

Bakhita Nyanut heard the gunshots and stood up to take water to General Doka. She panicked and almost poured the water.

"Friendly fire," General Doka said, and smiled broadly as he took the cup of water from Nyanut.

"We will have a few captives by the end of today if all goes according to plan," he added, and gulped down the water.

"Blue, this is Amara, Over." The radio said in General Doka's hand.

"Go ahead Amara, over"

"Enemy has refused to surrender, retreated into the warship cabin and ready to engage us, over."

As if to confirm Amara's report, heavy guns and automatic ones began to scream in the direction of the river. General Doka could hear the distinctive sound of a 20mm Oerlikon.

"Put the artillery unit in position, block their retreat and engage, over." General Doka said.

"Wilco over."

"Roger Out."

For the next few hours, the artillery unit pounded at the warship which replied with fire of its own.

* * *

Lieutenant Bol Deng of the artillery unit kept his cool as much as he could, ignoring the fact that he could get killed or lose his hearing. He believed that when his day came, he would die regardless of his cautions and therefore, battle presented a unique chance find out whether it was your day or not. If it was your day, you never made it back to base, if it was not, you returned without so much as a scratch.

Today, he hovered over his men. Before him were artillery guns spaced at a distance from each other. There was a D-30 122mm howitzer thundering away and spitting multiple empty shells, as well as 2A18 (D-20) 152mm towed gun-howitzers, all soviet made. They produced ear splitting sounds to scare enemies even miles away. Lieutenant Bol moved among these guns, his hears plugged with little pieces of cloth to act as sound stoppers.

From the warship, the Sudan Armed forces had their artillery pieces spitting fire, too accurate for Bol's liking. Twice, they barely missed the SPLA artillery guns by mere yards, shrapnel cutting and injuring few of the artillery unit members, but Bol was patient.

His guns might miss many times, but he knew that should one shell hit the warship, the crew would either surrender or shoot faster and deplete their ammunition. Either way, the result would be surrender. Lieutenant Bol watched the exchange from close range. Five hours after firing the three warning shots at the warship, the first artillery shell struck.

The navy men on the warship stopped shooting and raised a white flag. Peace. Bol breathed in deeply and exhaled. Not yet, he cautioned himself. He gave a thumbs up sign for one of his soldiers to go on to the riverbank and beckon the warship to anchor there. Sergeant Rou volunteered.

* * *

Sergeant Rou walked to the riverbank, the breeze blowing over his face. He slung his gun over his shoulder and made signs to the warship crew to anchor at the opposite shore. The warship didn't move.

Sergeant Rou made the signs again and the ship began to slide towards the banks. Rou had it in his mind to flog some of those soldiers aboard the warship later but then, he wasn't the leader here, and he was glad. He felt terrible today. He had been dreaming of Fatima and that always made for a terrible day, the pain always came back.

The navy men anchored their ship, coming out of the cabins one at a time with hands held over their heads, to stand on the deck. Lieutenant Bol Deng ordered his men to check the captives.

The men led by Sergeant Rou hit the captives with the butts of their guns and kicked them. Some of the captives already had blood flowing freely from their noses.

"No torture!" Lieutenant Bol commanded half heartedly, but the truth was he wanted his men to use more than their gun butts. In fact, he wanted them to kill the bastards, but the order had come already from the leadership to arrest the captives and bring them to base alive. Killing them would be insubordination, and insubordination was death. Bol couldn't die yet, he needed to get to Aweil, avenge Garang, and get back to his old man in the village. His old man had called him a useless son and Bol needed to show him what he had become; 'A beny wearing stars in the SPLA'.

After setting the warship ablaze, the rebels tied the hands of their captives behind their back and marched them back to base, kicking them as they moved. Alor Biong hated the horror and pain he saw in their eyes because it reminded him of the faces of his people back in Abyei. He wanted to feel good because the Arabs were the ones experiencing that now, but Alor knew that while a few Arab soldiers were experiencing this in the South, multitudes of Southerners were experiencing worse conditions in the North and in the cities across the South.

The base was a place haphazardly set up under a dense canopy, and the commanders of the battalion sat under a tree.

When General Doka saw the captives, he said, "SPLA oyee!" and the soldiers joined in. Alor joined in the shouting and sergeant Rou stood quietly. Alor spotted Bakhita Nyanut bringing water to the commanders and his heart skipped a beat. Don't be Stupid! he cautioned himself, but it was useless. As soon as Nyanut left to go back to where the ladies were cooking, Alor found himself following. His heart was in control, not his brain.

CHAPTER 21

"Which of the Dinka dialects is that, by the way?" Alor asked after introduction, "I have difficulty differentiating dialects. It's only the Twic dialect I can recognize. I can neither recognize nor differentiate those of Thäy."

"You don't recognize dialects of who?" Nyanut inquired

"Thäy." Alor repeated

"You've lost me. I don't follow. Who are Thäy?"

"Oh sorry, I forgot it is a term used mostly and probably only in Abyei. Thäy are the other Dinka subsections so long as they are not Twic or Ngok Abyei."

"That's really a demeaning word. Thäy as in just Thäy," Nyanut said and laughed, "you Ngak are really lost. People say that a lot in Aweil and I believe them now."

"So, you are Nyan Miluet. Nice to meet you and no we are not lost, our dialect still resembles original Dinka unlike yours."

The conversation took place under a tree a little bit far away from the base where Nyanut had gone to pick some firewood, and Alor had followed.

131

"You know, they say my grandfather was perhaps the greatest chief in the Southern Sudan if not the whole Sudan. He had 250 wives and he never even had to date half of them. His wives were only too happy to date on his behalf."

"Oh."

"Yes," Alor said, "To this day the entire area of the nine Ngok Dinka chiefdoms is called Abyein Deng Kuol."

"Oh, you mean him. I heard a lot of songs about his greatness back in my village," Nyanut said, sounding sad, but Alor did not notice.

"Yes, it's him," Alor said excitedly, "some people say he sold our land but that's not true. Such people do not understand that protecting oneself sometimes involves using your head. My grandpa used his."

"Nyanut," the voice of Aker Deng better known as 'Old man' among the soldiers came through the woods.

"Go," Nyanut told Alor.

"Tomorrow. Same time, same place." Alor said as he disappeared into the thickets

"Maybe," Nyanut said, almost in whisper. She carried her firewood and made for the base, pretending not to have heard Aker's call.

"Why did you have to go so far? There's dry wood all over the place," She said, and Nyanut murmured something about the wood being plentier deeper in the forest.

***

General Yusif Doka watched Lieutenant colonel Martin fume over the radio and dump it to the ground like red hot iron. Lieutenant Colonel Martin had been in communication with the central command, and from where General Doka stood, he could hear the voice from the other end, broken.

"...deliver the captives safely to Wau.... Geneva convention.... "

"Geneva convention, can you hear that? When did rebel forces become party to it? Nevermind that if the government forces capture us, it would be firing squad faster than you can say Deng Nhial."

General Doka agreed with him. He wanted to execute the captives Anyanya style, but the political commissars attached to Rhino by the central command argued that it would be a great political goal if they adhered to the Geneva convention. Apart from becoming the first rebel army to do so world-wide, the SPLA would also win admiration and support from the international community. The commissars had hard time convincing the commanders though. At long last, the point was dropped in favour of following the central commands.

* * *

Alor Biong waited under the tree, pacing up and down, willing Nyanut to turn up but she didn't. What had he done? Had he bored her on their first meeting? Alor found himself thinking he had.

Stupid, stupid!

He turned and walked back into the woods.

He heard some wood breaking behind him followed by the hooting of an owl and Alor turned instinctively and surveyed the area with his eyes. It reminded him of Kiirkou and his first gun and his uncle, Captain Kuol. He took a step forward again and the owl hooted again, louder and nearer. Alor instinctively unslung his gun from his shoulder and cocked. He pointed it at the thickets and waited, crouching low.

"Put away your gun muony Ngok, you will scare the wits out of me," Nyanut said, laughing as she marched out of her hiding place, hands raised high over her head in a mock gesture of 'I surrender and I'm unarmed'.

Alor chuckled despite himself.

"Nyan Miluet, you almost scared the piss out of me."

"Say, you didn't wet that trouser, did you?" Nyanut pursed her lips and wrinkled her nose.

"Not yet. Had you stayed out of sight a second longer, I would have released enough piss to flood this forest."

"What a coward," Nyanut teased, "I prefer honest cowards to dishonest brave people. It always turns out they are faking it. "

Alor felt butterflies flutter in his stomach. She likes me, he told himself. The two sat down and naturally, like it has been with women since time immemorial, Nyanut wanted to tell him her story. Alor listened as she spoke. It was a long speech punctuated by sobbing and tears rolling down her checks. Alor told her it was ok, but it was not, and he knew it. It would never be ok, so long as master Abdallah lived.

When the two finally returned to the base, they found that orders had been given to move. They did not know where they were going, but they were heading towards Bahr el Ghazal. Nyanut felt strangely happy, she was going home and every step she took brought her closer to master Abdallah. She had a gun, and it was master Abdallah's turn to dread meeting her.

***

Sergeant Rou stood behind Alor and kept grinning. He watched as Alor stole glances at Nyanut, who walked in the company of women. Interestingly, Nyanut stole glances at Alor too and the way she glanced at Alor reminded Rou of his long-lost love with Fatima.

Rou knew what was coming. Most young recruits assumed that the government forces would surrender as easily as the ones on the warship had. "How wrong they are!" Sergeant Rou said under his breath. The fact was the battle had not yet started, far from it.

Nobody enters war and comes out completely unscathed. One might survive, but one's loved ones do not all survive unless under special circumstances.

They had been moving for days and Sergeant Rou had lost count of the exact number. Those who knew Equatoria said they were in Terekeka. The grass in the countryside had become short and the topography flat. To Rou, it was more like Bahr el Ghazal than Equatoria. Equatoria was supposed to have thick forests, and hills not as so flat as this. He wouldn't help but feel that those who divided the South into three regions had missed this fact and Terekeka should have been Bahr el Ghazal.

* * *

The battalion camped at the outskirts of Aweirial and divided into platoons.

General Doka, who was the chief of operations moved around camp, thoughtful. He had sent two platoons into the villages around Aweirial to gather intel and to engage the government troops briefly, leading them to believe that the SPLA was not capable of overrrunning the towns. So far nothing had been heard from the two platoons and it had now been two days since the platoons had left. General Doka had lost radio connection with them on the first day, and faint gunshots had been heard, but otherwise there was nothing more. The General feared the worst.

"Walk with me," General Doka told First Lieutenant Awan Bol, who followed him immediately, keeping a respectable distance.

"In what state is your platoon?" General Doka asked.

"Quite good, and buzzing to get involved in the action, General," lieutenant Awan said.

"They will get their chance soon," said General Doka, holding his long grey-stricken beard thoughtfully, "we will give the two platoons one more day. If they are not in touch by that time, you and your platoon will go. Prepare."

"Yes, General."

"If it happens that you and your platoon should go on the mission tomorrow, you are Alpha Bravo, and I am Yankee Delta, for purposes of radio communication."

"Yes, sir."

General Doka watched the man go and sighed. He found it hard to think. Part of him knew that the two platoons had probably been annihilated, but another part of him was optimistic. Maybe their radios malfunctioned, but two radios to malfunction at the same time was just too much coincidence.

General Doka wandered to the outskirts of their new base and his escort followed closely.

"Get me Second Lieutenant Bol Deng of the artillery unit," he said to his escort, and one of the three left to look for him.

The soldier soon returned with the Lieutenant.

"How's your unit?" General Doka asked the lieutenant.

"Itching for some action, I believe. They think their guns are getting cold."

"Tomorrow, there might be a mission for you. Pick out twelve of your best men. You will be taking no heavy artillery pieces, only a Toyota pick up and AK47s. Heavy guns would slow you down and yet this mission depends on haste."

"Yes, sir!" lieutenant Bol Deng said but, in his heart, he fumed. An artillery unit going out to fight without the artillery guns is like a fish going to fight out of water. Dead before the battle even begins.

"For this mission," General Doka said, bringing Bol out of his thoughts, "You will be Blue and I, yellow for purposes of radio communication."

"Yes, sir! " lieutenant Bol Deng said, already feeling headache. He hated his boss.

CHAPTER 22

"Alpha Bravo, this is Blue, over." A voice said from the receiver.

"Go ahead Blue, Over," Alpha Bravo said.

"Alpha Bravo, enemy tracked three kilometers West, break. Take cover three kilometers East at Mike Kilo. Read back, over."

"I will read back now: enemy tracked Three kilometers West. Take cover three kilometers East at Mike Kilo, over."

"Correct, over."

"Roger, out."

Alpha Bravo put down the receiver and kicked the side of the front car tyre.

"Damn it!" he swore loudly and reached for the cigarette that was stuck behind his ear. He lit it and puffed.

"Three kilometers East, men. Move, now!" He took his seat in a green open-roof Toyota pick-up next to the driver. The Toyota pick-up was mounted with a 20mm Oerlikon gun with a long ammunition belt hanging from it. Inside the Toyota pick-up were boxes of ammunition and branches laden with green leaves tied to its sides for camouflage. It moved slowly in the mud. Alpha Bravo continued to puff his cigarette. Around the car, his platoon jogged lightly, boots sticking into the mud from time to time and quiet as shadows.

He had expressly ordered them not to sing because the enemy had been tracked as being too near to them. He remembered vividly what he had seen of the two platoons sent before them, food for the vultures. Most of them had had their throats slit, taken unawares in their camp at night. Some of Alpha Bravo's men had thrown up at the sight of their butchered colleagues. Alpha Bravo removed a piece of paper from his pocket and studied its contents. The plan that was all but abandoned now.

His mind kept replaying the conversation he had had with General Doka the morning before he had led his platoon towards Mingkaman:

"I don't like this. They've out witted us. They seem to be waiting for us in well laid out ambushes. The two platoons might be wiped out for all we know. Something is not right here. There's something we are missing," General Doka said, pacing up and down, "what do you think lieutenant?"

"Someone is either talking, or our plans are not well laid."

General Doka had patted him on the back,

"I like to hear my thoughts from others Lieutenant. I'm glad I'm entrusting you with this mission. You and I are of like mind, and I believe you'll bring me news of the capture of Yirol town by this time tomorrow. I'll also send a second platoon after you, their goal being to gather intel on enemy movements and relay them to you promptly. It will be led by Second Lieutenant Bol Deng, Blue for radio communication purposes only. See why your pick of men is very important? The entire Batallion depends on you."

"General, what happens if more soldiers surrender seeing as we are already burdened by more than two dozen captives?"

General Doka clenched his teeth. Of course, he had expected that question to arise sooner, but that didn't make it easier to answer.

"Kill them," He said between clenched teeth. Don't say later 'I told you so', he added in his head.

"Take this, " General Doka handed a piece of paper over to 1st lieutenant Awan, "that's the plan. It's not meant to be rigid though."

Alpha Bravo awoke from his thoughts to find that he had made a paper boat out of Doka's plan. He hastily folded it and placed it back into his front shirt pocket.

Reports were coming in thick from the central command. The Southern axis battalions had captured Owiny-Kibul and fought as far as Gemezia, stopping fifty kilometers South of Bor town. The Eastern axis had also captured the Boma plateau while the central command itself had captured Jekou. Even the Northern axis had captured Maban. Only the Bahr el Ghazal remained untouched, not for want of trying, but the SAF seemed to read their moves. It was almost like they were following a script.

Damn it. Alpha Bravo clenched his teeth in rage.

"Kariak-chak" Something clicked in the nearby thickets. It took Alpha bravo a few seconds to place the sound, mostly out of disbelief than because of the sound's unfamiliarity, it was a gun being cocked.

"Take cover!" Alpha Bravo ordered.

The entire platoon went down flat on their belies, guns at the ready and, as if that was what they had been waiting for, the enemy poured out of the thickets, directing a hail of bullets at the land cruiser on which the 20mm Oerlikon gun stood idle.

"Retreat into the trees!" Alpha Bravo barked. The squad made for the trees and two men fell in the attempt. One of the soldiers turned in the opposite direction and made for the Land Cruiser. Alpha Bravo glanced at him, dumfounded. It was the small man whom the commander had promoted to the rank of Sergeant. You are a dead man, Alpha Bravo spat.

The Sergeant jumped onto the car, got hold of the 20mm Oerlikon, and opened fire. The 20 mm Oerlikon danced. Alpha Bravo watched from where he was taking cover. He would never forget what he saw and would tell it years later to new recruits and to his friends. The 20mm Oerlikon spat fire as it spans in arcs, swallowing the ammunition belt. The enemy bullets seemed to dodge the sergeant rather than him dodging them. To Alpha Bravo, everything seemed wrong, very wrong, but he didn't care.

"Attack!" Alpha Bravo commanded his men, before one man could take the entire glory of a victory alone. The platoon attacked;two men short but with a high morale. In the Land cruiser, their sergeant danced with the machine gun, spraying bullets, and the enemy fell before them. The platoon emerged from the trees, where they had been taking cover and started firing at the enemy, shouting jubilantly,

"Katiba Rhino oyee!"

"SPLA oyee!"

The enemy, having lost more men than were still alive, tried to make a tactical withdrawal, and more of them fell. A few managed to run pell-mell into the trees where the platoon could not get them. Alpha Bravo breathed deeply and exhaled, hardly believing his platoon had won, and not only that, but they had also won the first battle by the Sudan People's Liberation Army on the Bahr el Ghazal front, and he was their leader. He imagined what it would be like to appear in history books in the future, 'The platoon underthe command of First Lieutenant Awan Bol entirely wiped out two platoons of the Sudan Armed Forces at Mingkaman. This marked the first victory on the Bahr el Ghazal front.' Short and sweet. There would be no mention of the stupid sergeant and his stupid antics. Alpha Bravo loved that stupid sergeant and wanted him as part of his entourage after his promotion.

* * *

General Doka sat in a green land cruiser pick-up. The main thrust of the of rhino was headed to Yirol town. That hadn't been part of the plan, but plans are made to be changed where results cannot sufficiently be achieved with the original plan. General Doka would have loved to call what was now being executed 'plan B' but it was not. This was simply a plan out of no where, a 'plan X' Doka decided.

The artillery unit set up their pieces a few kilometers short of the town and pounded the government positions for an hour until General Doka gave the signal to attack on the ground.

Alor walked towards Nyanut and bade her goodbye, before running into battle with the rest of the soldiers.

Shouts of "Katiba Rhino Oyee! SPLA oyee," filled the air.

Smoke rose thick over the town as houses were set ablaze and the the artillery guns pounded. The government forces in town tried to dig in and defend their positions but it proved futile, and the town fell. Locals waited outside their homes cheering the commanders of the forces as they drove into town in land cruisers. Lieutenant Colonel Martin stood in his land cruiser and waved to the locals.

"SPLA oyee!" he shouted, and the locals picked up from there.

"Athielei oyeei" they repeated.

General Doka watched coolly. He knew the the real driving force behind this victory, the two platoons he had sent out, and he was not about to forget them. He discussed his idea with the overall commander and the two lieutenants who led those platoons were to be promoted to Major and Captain respectively. The two platoons entered Yirol town at noon to be welcomed by more jubilations from their colleagues and the locals.

* * *

Alor watched sergeant Rou jump down from a speeding land cruiser and rushed towards him. He embraced Alor like a young brother. The two men looked at each other and laughed. It was good to be alive, especially when there was so much death around you.

Yirol is a funny little town, Alor thought. Young adolescent girls moved around naked, and he made a mental note: when I return to Abyei, I will tell my people that they have missed it by a wide margin. The Agar are not man eaters, but something else entirely.

"We are supposed to woo them like that? I mean what do we want? It's already before us," one Soldier told his friends, and everybody was rolling in laughter. None dared touch the girls. Everything was before them and they could see it, but Lieutenant Colonel Martin had decreed that anyone fond guilty of rape would be given to the firing squad.

The two were trying to sit down and make themselves comfortable when gunfire broke out at the outskirts of the town. The army was making a last-ditch attempt to reassert control. Naturally Alor, Sergeant Rou and other soldiers ran in the direction with guns at the ready, but the enemy had already been stopped and driven towards Terekeka. Victory songs filled the air. Alor and those who had arrived joined the celebrations.

One moment, everybody was singing, the next a single gunshot was heard. How it had somehow managed to thread its way among so many people, to find it's way to Sergeant Rou, Alor would never know. There was no explanation.

"It's his day" they said.

That was outright unacceptable to Alor. Why this day of all days? He had asked repeatedly, and no answers ever came.

Alor stood over the body of Sergeant Rou, everything around him seemed to have stopped. He opened his mouth to scream but nothing came out.

This time, the bullet hadn't been deflected by the magazines around the sergeant's waist. It had gotten him right on the left side of his chest, where his heart is. He fell limp as soon as the bullet hit, no scream, no nothing. Blood gushed from the wound and Sergeant Rou was no more. The bandits of Kiirkou were being wiped out, just one of them left. Alor screamed.

CHAPTER 23

Bakhita Nyanut felt excitement welling up in her. She retraced her footsteps and was once again in rol cuol akol, the famed forest of sunset. Her mind had begun to calculate the time left till she could see Aweil again. She put it at twenty days of nonstop walking, but she wasn't sure, she suspected it could be less and the last time she had covered this distance was on her way to Bilpam. It was barely a year since she undertook that journey but seemed like ages had passed.

Her heart beat faster when she imagined Master Abdallah's face when she finally got him. She wanted to see the real thing, to hit his stupid face with the butt of her gun. She wanted vengeance for herself, for her family, for Makom village.

"Alor Biong," Alor heard his name called on the parade at their base in Cueibet. It was General Doka. He came forward and the General placed one star on the shoulder of his uniform and buttoned it. He was now Second Lieutenant Alor Biong. Ordinarily, this should have made him happy, but it did not. He had left his family to join the revolution, but what had he gained?

An uncle was now dead, his colleagues were dead, Sergeant Rou was dead and maybe soon he would lose own life. He mourned for his Sergeant, for his uncle, and for himself. Wouldn't it have been better if he had simply just stayed in Abyei, and fished frogs from the Nyamora? One thing was sure though, if he hadn't gone to Bilpam, he wouldn't have met Nyanut. Not a chance.

"Walk with me," General Doka told Alor after the parade. Alor obliged.

"Congratulations," General Doka said.

"Thank you."

"I understand how you feel after losing your friend, but that's the curse of being a soldier at war, weeping. The only people who will be spared weeping are those who will be wept for."

Alor nodded quietly. He knew and understood, but knowledge did not take away the pain. He could feel his heart pump faster and would glance behind him, expecting to see Sergeant Rou standing there like he had always done, but he wasn't there. He had been buried in some unmarked grave down in Yirol town, although the man he had buried was Captain Rou, after being promoted posthumously to that rank. Alor would have to look for the grave once the whole South had been liberated.

"We move on Tonj tomorrow. Your primary work will be to lead my entourage. Make sure you are well rested. For this mission, we want to minimize casualties from our side as much as possible. "

"Yes, sir!" Alor said

"They won't put up much resistance in Tonj. Wau is their prize to protect, so they will likely withdraw into Wau and dig in. Prepare for the great chase."

Second Lieutenant Alor Biong Saluted and walked off.

***

Bakhita Nyanut watched Alor come towards her and realized that she loved him. With his slender build and hair, which encroached on the forehead, she thought he was beauty personified. She had him and felt guilty because he deserved better. He deserved someone who was not a used wretch like herself, but he wanted her, even with the knowledge about her past. She wouldn't stop him, that would be like rejecting God's blessings. Alor was itching to have a go at Master Abdallah and had agreed to come to Aweil with her. She had tried to dissuade him, but he would have none of it. His dreams were big, and she approved of them because these dreams had her at the center. Today, those who wanted to go as far as Aweil. Nyanut, Alor and Second Lieutenant Bol Deng, who had been promoted to Captain had a meeting. The rebels wanted to stop in Tonj after overrunning it, but these three wanted to proceed northwards to settle old scores.

"So," Alor said, "how do we make it there? Passing through Wau with our weapons, even if concealed, is a no."

"Kuajok. We'll pass through Kuajok and head towards Akon, from there we can get into Northern Bahr el Ghazal state via Aweil South. Once there, it's a matter of walking straight into Aweil town or anywhere we might think of," Bol said, drawing a badly deformad map of Sudan and marking the route he was proposing. Nyanut looked on, reminded of how young and ignorant she was. She had no idea where Bol had drawn or the places he was talking about. All she knew was Aweil town.

The trio's meeting ended prematurely when a whistle blast called the rebels to assemble. Apparently, the government forces had decided to take the rebels unawares. It was time for action. Alor hurriedly put on his battle gear and ordered the other five junior officers to do the same.

He did not see most of the battle because he was protecting

General Doka, whose job was mostly formulating battle strategies and giving orders from afar. Nevertheless, the sound of the artillery guns and the Kalashnikov rifles did not cease for five hours. The two armies had met at the border between Gok and Tonj.

"The men are losing morale," General Doka said, "time to reinforce them."

He blew a whistle and a hundred reserve forces assembled. It was time to finish the job. The reserve forces marched to battle with Commander Yusif Doka and his entourage in their midst.

***

Alor Biong turned left, then right, then left again. The battle was in full swing, and he had lost General Doka and the other five members of his entourage. A bullet whistled over Alor's head, just an inch away from his hair. Another bullet razed his cheek and Alor felt blood trickle down, but he did not touch it. He leaned behind a tree and breathed deeply, then ducked down in a trench, belly-first and aimed at an approaching horse. A talisman bearer. Alor pulled the trigger and the bullet hit the horse's neck. The beast jumped up and fell back to the ground, instantly breaking the neck of its rider.

Alor targeted another oncoming horse and pulled the trigger. It neighed madly and dropped its rider where the man fell onto his knees and made a run for it. Alor followed him with his gun, but he couldn't get a good target. He hadn't learnt how to hit a moving target, but he pulled the trigger anyway. The man fell limb and Alor had become a sharpshooter without knowing it.

"The General, save the General!" A cry went up on the left plank of the battlefield.

"No!" Alor screamed. It was happening again. He ran to where the cry came from. General Doka with his entourage, or what was left of them, were in something like a cleverly made ambush. They were encircled, and between them were enemy bullets and scattered trees.

As Alor ran towards them, a bullet hit the General squarely on the chest.

The old man fell, screaming like a child. Alor had seen this before. It was bad luck, and he was its catalyst. Everyone in his charge seemed to die.

The enemy retreated and the rebels gave a chase but not Alor. He went to General Doka, or what was left of him. When Alor reached him, the old General was still alive. He slipped a notebook into Alor's hand. Alor slipped it into his pocket, but he didn't need books, he needed to save the General's life.

General Doka soon fell into a deep, eternal sleep. Tonj was captured that evening and General Doka was buried with honour, his body wrapped in the SPLA flag. Alor felt guilty. Somehow, he had let the General get killed. He blamed himself but if that pained him, the man who succeeded Doka pained him more. Captain Kon Lual had been promoted to the rank of Major and made head of operations for Rhino. Alor felt resentful towards the man for everything he had done to Nyanut.

* * *

It had been a week since General Doka's demise and Tonj had been completely secured. Alor kept fingering his bag. Packing and unpacking. He felt it was time to get going North but Nyanut and Captain Bol had not yet given the signal to move. He felt something bulging in a shirt pocket, removed it and stared at it for a long time. It was the notebook General Doka had slipped into his hand just before his death. Alor placed his bag aside, leaned against the wall in his small hut and opened the book. The first two pages were filled with untidy writing, letters spaced so far apart that it was hard to read. Alor's reading had improved since he learnt radio communication back in Bilpam. He read the first untidy words in capital letters, probably meant to be the title, and the text that followed. The title looked eerily like something out of the Bible.

THE WORDS OF DOKA, SON OF KENYI WHO HAS SEEN IT ALL.

Since mutiny of August '55, I have been close to the center of affairs in this country. They call me the Lion of Immatong, but what happened in those mountains was pure luck. I'm no hero, but if there is one thing I have become, it's an expert at recognizing this vicious cycle. The cycle of hatred.

A time is coming when an agreement will be signed between the government and the leadership of this movement. When that happens, money will come in and many of these things will happen if not all.

There will be a struggle for power as the ideals of new Sudan will evaporate and the structure of this movement will come crumbling down. It will be as if this movement has never had a structure at all.

The fighters of this movement will not reap from their handiwork, prodigal sons who were either working with the enemy or have gone to stay safe in Europe and America will come back in their dozens and the reigns of power will be handed over to them. They will eat what was meant for the citizens and should anything be left over; they'll take and give it to their foreign friends.

The people of Southern Sudan will remain second class citizens even if a New Sudan comes to pass. Only a few will eat, the rest will starve or remain refugees for generations.

The people will defend their abusive leaders furiously and in this furious defense will sprout the seeds of the next cycle of hate. The abusive leaders will continue to hold power, and the cycle will keep recurring. Many will die until a group will finally see what I have seen so far. Namely, That this is a cycle and to end a cycle, we must be willing to give up a lot.

It's not for me to say what must be given up. When the time comes, when the time is right. My dear reader, you will know.

Nothing is new.

Alor Biong finished reading and put the little book back into the pocket, repacked his bag and went to look for his partners in the crime he was about to commit.

CHAPTER 24

It was May again, the month Nyanut escaped from her abusive master; the sixteenth day of the month. Among the soldiers of the Sudan People's Liberation Army, the day was known by its Arabic equivalent: Sit-thashar Mayo, or just the SPLA day. It reminded them of the the day the first bullet was shot to launch the struggle. Soldiers shot up celebratory bullets, but not Nyanut. It was May and she was escaping again, not away from abuse like before, but instead to go and settle scores. With her were four men: Second Lieutenant Alor Biong and Captain Bol Deng with his two escorts.

The deserting party began to move as the celebration was heating up and the shooting began. They moved in darkness. The moon had not yet come up and Captain Bol Deng said it was better that way. By the time it came up, he hoped they would be far away from the command base. By the following day, Bol said they would be out of Tonj South and deep into Tonj North, just few miles from Gogrial East.

Deserting was not an unknown thing in the SPLA and many deserted everyday. Some got caught in the act while others were apprehended from their home villages. They were warned, punished and given a second chance to serve, but if they did eventually escape again, and were unlucky and caught a second time, they were executed.

The five moved in shadows. Nyanut had argued against the wisdom of bringing the two security escorts along, but Captain Bol Deng would have none of it. How else was his father supposed to know that he, the useless son, had become a 'beny'?

The group moved with a sense of purpose, their experienced feet raising unseen dust on the dark road. They avoided settlements whenever possible.

They soon understood that making it out of Tonj was no easy task. They travelled the whole night and the next day with only little rests in between, yet they only made it to the outskirts of Tonj by the evening of the second day. Nyanut knew Bol had never travelled in Warrap, all his talk was just based on assumption.

* * *

The deserting party made its way through Gogrial East county. Alor Biong walked behind Nyanut, hovering protectively over her. Remotely in his mind, he knew that somewhere North of where he now walked was Kiirkou and beyond that, Abyei. Abyei with its suffering population, Abyei which was beyond help for now. He forced himself not to think about it and watched Nyanut move, her new civilian clothes with a 'top' thrown over them made her even more beautiful.

The party hid their guns in sacks which they carried over their shoulders. They arrived at a place with great green pastures and herds upon herds of cattle grazing on it.

"Behold, the great Toch Apuk of legend," Bol exclaimed.

Nyanut watched with fascination the great, seemingly endless green grassland and remembered the stories her mother used to tell her. In these stories, the herdsmen always went to Apuk with their cattle and a young girl who had been left behind would try to follow them. A lion would meet the girl en route and try to eat the girl, but the girl would challenge him to a dancing competition. The two would dance until the lion's heart burst and it died.

Tears rolled down Nyanut's cheeks as she recalled her mother. Her mother who had treated her like a princess, her mother whose life the Arabs cut short. Nyanut's heart longed for revenge. In the meantime, she savoured the smell of cattle, a smell almost lost to her memory. The party walked and walked until they were out of Gogrial East, and every step taken brought them ever closer to Kuajok.

"There will certainly be a military presence in Kuajok, seeing as it's the only real town in Gogrial," Alor said.

"Of course," Captain Bol Deng replied, "that's where our sacks will come in handy. We'll need a little more than just sacks though. We need something to put into those sacks before someone finds out about our lethal luggage."

"Sshhhh. I can hear people coming this way," Captain Bol said. Alor and the rest listened. True, there was what sounded like a bicycle caravan on the move. The group decided not to hide but to continue like another group of civilians taking their produce to Market in Kuajok.

The bicycle riders drew closer until the crew could see them. There were Four bicycles loaded with sacks and Captain Bol called out to the riders,

"What are you carrying to the market brothers?"

"Groundnuts," said the lead rider.

"Guns out," Captain Bol whispered. The five deserters yanked their rifles out of the sacks in unison and pointed them at the riders.

"Stand still," Captain Bol ordered them. They told the riders to choose between a return on foot to Gogrial East, or death. The wise men chose the former and made a run for it.

The sacks really did contain groundnuts. The five put their guns securely into two of the sacks, dropped one sack, and took the bicycles along with three sacks. Two contained guns and some groundnuts and one was full of groundnuts only. Captain Bol and his two bodyguards rode the bicycles loaded with the sacks while Nyanut rode on a bicycle with Alor.

"If at anytime anyone should check us, leave him to me. My sack contains nothing apart from groundnuts. That's what he'll check first and hopefully, won't want to check any more of the sacks," Captain Bol said.

The party then rode like their lives depended on it towards Kuajok and in a way, their lives really did depend on their haste.

* * *

Kuajok was teeming with people, both soldiers and civilians. The deserters passed most of the town without any incident but that changed as soon as they made it to the outskirts of the town. On a path to Panliet Awan, there was a checkpoint they hadn't noticed. By the time they noticed it, it was already too late to turn back. Regime soldiers stood by the roadside, guns at the ready. They were doing a thorough check of all Southern travellers because the Anyanya two of Northern Bahr el Ghazal had attacked the town few days before.

"Shit!" Captain Bol Deng cursed. Alor tried to branch to another path.

"That'll only get us killed," the Captain cautioned him. "They have seen us already. Let them check us. Hopefully, it will be only my sack."

"Get down the bicycles and open those sacks," a soldier barked at them as soon as they neared the checkpoint.

Captain Bol Deng opened sack and told the other two to open theirs, but to put enough groudnuts on top so the guns wouldn't protrude.

"Step aside," the soldier said, pushing Bol roughly to the side of the road. Bol signalled to the others to step aside too and let the soldier do his work.

We are dead, Bol thought with complete regret. Was he going to die without avenging Garang and not proving his old man wrong?

The soldier peered into Bol's sack, put his hand into it and stirred the groundnuts. It was as if he knew what he was looking for, and how it had been hidden. He found nothing and moved to the next sack. Bol turned away, resigned to their inevitable fate.

* * *

Alor Biong watched the soldier walk to the second sack with a mixture of fear and regret. He wanted to grab Nyanut's hand and run into the bushes with hope that the soldiers wouldn't shoot at them, but he knew deep in his heart that such hope was futile. The soldier reached the sack and opened it. Alor shuddered but at that moment, guns begun to scream in the nearby trees.

The Anyanya Two had attacked again.

In the confusion that followed, Alor and one of Captain Bol's security escorts reached for the two sacks that contained their guns and pulled them into the nearby thicket. The Arab soldiers had panicked and retreated into the Kuajok center to get reinforcements. The deserters lay in the bushes until after the battle was long gone. They later heard that it had been a skirmish, a diversion from the real attack that was on another side of the town. The five were happy, it saved their lives.

After that They travelled in the bushes until they entered Panliet Awan a day later.

"Tomorrow, we'll be in Akon and thereafter, Aweil South!" A visibly excited Captain Bol Deng announced.

CHAPTER 25

"Pan cit America," Captain Bol Deng said with a broad smile on his face, when they finally crossed into Aweil South from Awan. For Bol and many other people from Aweil, the land of Aweil is like America. It is the highest praise the native people could bestow on the land of their fathers.

For Alor Biong, there was nothing worthy of praise that he could see. It was all rough, dry land that seemed infertile and unfit for cultivation. There were also no pasture lands as rich as Toch Apuk that he could see, but he nevertheless understood Bol's reverence for his land. He knew he would say the same things about Abyei even though some parts of it were a semi-desert, unfit for cultivation. Alor wanted to live in Aweil though and hoped to Christ it was indeed like America if only vaguely.

***

Bakhita Nyanut stared at the vast barren white piece of land. There was no grass even though the rain was falling. They were in Panthou, and the barren piece of land they looked at was what would later become famous Panthou airstrip. As vast as the place was, it did not distract her. Her mind was on one thing and one thing only: how to get master Abdallah now that she was a day's walk away from Aweil town.

She had thought of revenge so much that she had overlooked just how hard it would be to exact revenge in a government-controlled town, where the slightest sound that resembled a gun sound would attract soldiers. It was even worse that the revenge would be against an Arab. Suddenly, the revenge she had dreamed of seemed far fetched.

"I think we should go to Pariak and stay there," Nyanut said to Alor who sat next to her, deep in thought.

"What about master Abdallah?" Alor asked, coming out of his thoughts.

"Let him be," Nyanut replied with tears flowing freely down her cheeks.

"Nobody is going to chicken out. Abdallah must pay for his sins; he must suffer like his religion says of sinners. You go to Pariak, I'll meet you there after settling the scores."

"No," Said Captain Bol Deng who had been listening to the conversation, "You two go to Pariak and I'll handle this business."

"Alright everyone, " Nyanut said, "Someone come up with a plan, because we can't go to Aweil town to kill an Arab without one. It's akin to suicide because he might get us before we get him."

"I suggest we track him for a week, see where he frequents, and kidnap him on the way. Once we know his routine, we'll be prepared enough," Captain Bol said.

"That sounds like something they do in Hollywood. I doubt its practicality. Besides how would we kidnap an obese man without a car?"

"The guy doesn't have any place he frequents. He spends his days between his house and his restaurant which are not very far apart. The Captain has got a good point. Tracking him is a must. We need to be sure he's at home if we are going to act while he's home," Nyanut explained.

"I suggest we plant a bomb on him," said Alor.

Captain Bol whistled.

"Another Hollywood idea. I thought we agreed such ideas won't do and I'm rather sad to also inform you that we have no bombs. Only hand grenades."

"Ok, at least we have a starting point, tracking him. We'll know what to do once we know where he will be and at what time," Nyanut said.

* * *

"Nyanut," said Captain Bol after traveling for few hours, "this is the famous Buoncuai. I hope you've heard of it."

"The rumoured home of famous spear masters, wizards and witches?"

"Yes," Bol said, "though with Muonyjieng, you'll never be sure of what is true and what is not unless you stay long enough here to find out on your own."

"Stay long enough? What if by the time you make your deductions, you already have a razor blade stuck in your heart put there by a witch or wizard?" She winced as if in pain.

Bol laughed.

"That is the risk one must take to find out the truth, I suppose."

They arrived in Aweil town two days later and Nyanut wore a top that covered most of her face. As for Bol, he needed no disguise because his beard had grown so long since he left Aweil town that he believed only his parents would recognize him and even they would have difficulty.

On their first day in Aweil town, Nyanut led the two body-guards and Alor into master Abdallah's neighborhood, and showed them the house and restaurant. The three were completely new in the town and nobody would stop to think twice about why they frequented a particular route. They calculated that their tracking would take a week before the they would finally establish the man's habits. The four went back to where they were stationed, a home at the outskirts of Aweil town. Real work would begin the following day.

*　*　*

Alor Biong entered the restaurant and took a seat only to find the restaurant packed with people. It was clearly thriving, and the dishes smelled excellent, but what immediately drew Alor's attention was the presence of a young girl, about Nyanut's age who sat quietly in the corner washing utensils.

He replaced her, Alor thought bitterly.

He felt rage burning in his heart. This master Abdallah was a pedophile.

"Abuk, is this how you wash the utensils?" A fat man entered the restaurant and barked at the young girl, throwing a plate. It missed her narrowly.

"No, master. It was just a mistake," the little girl said automatically.

Her voice was soft but she was not close to tears and Alor imagined she faced worse and that this particular episode was minor.

Alor Biong watched the brute of a man he had heard about from Nyanut. It seemed to him that her description of the man was flawed. Instead of saying the man is fat, she should have said that the man is a 'toad'.

Alor's order arrived but he left it uneaten. Master Abdallah stepped out of the restaurant and Alor followed a moment later. He held up a thumbs up sign, a pre-arranged signal to inform his colleagues that the target is on the move. After a few minutes, the two men met Alor in a corner.

"He went home directly, lieutenant," one of them told Alor. He nodded silently and the three went back to their base.

* * *

"The man is a brute, a pedophile and cannot, will not be allowed to live any longer," Alor Biong said enraged once back at the base, "It did not just happen to Nyanut. He's got another young girl and God knows what he makes her go through."

Nyanut covered her face with her hands and sobbed. Alor went closer to her and patted her shoulders.

"We are a bit late, but I promise, that young girl Abuk will be his last victim come what may."

The three kept tracking master Abdallah with the same result. The man went to the restaurant at eight o'clock in the morning and returned home at one o'clock in the afternoon using the same route.

There was only one question, where was he at one o'clock in the morning? Was he in his wife's room or Abuk's?

Nyanut assured them that the man would almost certainly be in Abuk's room. It was a risk they had to take, but Nyanut said that she was sure. They chose the D-Day.

When the D-Day came, the five put their guns in a sack and snuck into town. They pretended they were traders from Aweil

East who had come to sell fish to the town and had no where to stay for the night.

When it was a few minutes after midnight, Captain Bol glanced at his watch. It said it was a quarter past twelve. Master Abdallah's house was a ten-minute walk from where they were. Dogs had started to bark at the shadows.

Captain Bol glanced at his watch again.

"We get moving," he whispered to his campanions. They crept in the shadows towards master Abdallah's house, praying to their gods to blind anyone whom they might encounter, but they encountered no one. They reached the compound, and Nyanut pointed to the room that had once been hers.

Muffled screams came from the room.

Nyanut tensed and she could feel Bol roll his fists as he stood next to her. She slowly got her gun and quietly fixed the bayonet on the muzzle. The two bodyguards of Captain Bol stood sentry while Alor and Captain Bol walked to the door and knocked.

"Who's there?" master Abdallah inquired. At that moment, Captain Bol and Second Lieutenant Alor kicked the door.

Before the man could scream, Bol's hands were firmly around his mouth.

"Your death," Bakhita Nyanut answered and plunged the bayonet into master Abdallah's bosom. Blood sputtered onto the floor. Alor removed his torch and shone a beam of light towards Nyanut so the monster could see who had come.

His eyes widened as he succumbed to the wound. Nyanut went towards the little girl who had watched the episode with no emotion and hugged her tightly.

***

The four of them and the little girl made it to the outskirts of the town by walking in shadows and avoiding checkpoints. At the base, Bol announced that he would be leaving to Pan Apuoth that morning and he'd be taking Abuk with her. Nyanut and Alor said they were going Aweil West to find relatives of Nyanut. The little girl slept, carried on Alor's back, as they walked. Nyanut looked up at the night sky, and sighed, it was finally over.

Epilogue

2013- Kakuma Refugee Camp

"Baba, Baba. rin kua ä tou thin- our names are there." A young girl ran shouting towards a man in his late thirties who was repairing an armchair in the compound. The man had a goatee and his hair had begun to recede from the forehead, giving him a slightly bald look. The Harmattan had blown too much on his face and his lips seemed to be waiting to break.

"Shushu, our names are where?" The man inquired, patting the little girl on the back and playfully pinching her cheeks.

"Rin kua ä tou thin." she repeated innocently.

"Maan Achai, what is your daughter talking about?"

A woman emerged from the kitchen, seemingly distracted. The little girl rushed towards her as soon as she emerged.

"Mama, rin kua a tou thin," she said pointing towards large tents pitched somewhere closer to their house.

The woman thought for a moment and said, "Wun Achai, you need to check the notice board."

The man scratched his head, irritated at being disturbed in his work.

"Nyanut, don't tell me that after all these years you seriously believe we shall still be resettled somewhere in Europe or Australia. If they had wanted, they would have taken us ten years ago. Forget it." But the woman insisted he go and check.

The man stood up and began the long journey to the United Nations compound. It was December sixteenth and there were reports from the new nation of South Sudan that the cycle had begun again.

It had been two decades since Alor Biong deserted from the Sudan People's Liberation Army and had advanced his education somewhat. He kept reading and re-reading the little note General Doka had left him and was convinced that the old General hadn't been hallucinating. He and Nyanut had come to Kakuma at the beginning of the century and despite Nyanut's insistence on going back home, Alor had stubbornly resisted. There were times he was tempted to go back home and reap from the fruits of the struggle, like General Ayii Akol and many others had done, but something always seemed to stop him. Sometimes, it was sickness but most times it was Nyanut's recurrent miscariages.

As he walked to the United Nations compound turned, turned everything in his mind. The reports were scattered and most came through word of mouth. Alor knew that Kakuma would be full soon like it had been during the war. What he heard being whispered throughout the camp reminded Alor of bad scenes from the '91 split of SPLM/A. They said there were two major tribes at each other's throat, and the other tribes had to pick sides. Alor suspected there was more to it than just tribes because wars are always more complex.

It had been months since his TV, which had served him for about five years, broke down. He had taken it to the repair man but had no money to pay for the service. His efforts were directed towards feeding his family instead and the TV was still at the repair man's workshop.

Alor reached the UN compound to find people swarming the notice boards. Some jumped up as they spotted their names among those being resettled in Europe or Australia. Others walked away, visibly sad because their names weren't there. Alor made his way through by squeezing through people gently until he finally faced the notice board. He scanned through the list of those to be resettled in Australia but there were not very many names, just thirty. Alor used his index finger as a sort of stylus to point while he scanned through, searching for his family members' names. Then he saw them.

He stood staring at the names for a while, names arranged in order with numbers.

10- Alor Biong Deng
11- Bakhita Nyanut Garang
12- Achai Alor Biong

He turned his back to the notice board and made his way again through the crowd. Alor displayed not a single emotion. Of course he was happy, but a Dinka man does not display his emotions easily. He had to do something else before he could go home and tell Nyanut the good news.

He dipped his right hand in his trouser pocket and pulled out a green bank note for five hundred Kenyan shillings. He had meant to save it and add another five hundred for the coming Christmas but not anymore. He had good news and to celebrate and he was going to watch TV. He passed at the repair man's workshop and got his TV after pocketing the change.

***

"Baba kan- Father is there," little Achai said and ran towards her father who was returning with a box TV in his arms. She reached him and hugged his knees, and they both walked back home together.

Nyanut watched grimly as the pair reached home.

He's spent the little he had on repairing that stupid TV, she thought. Achai kept inspecting the TV with her child's curiosity. Nyanut could hear their neighbours celebrating because they had finally been relocated. Their generator, the one from which Nyanut and her family got electricity was started.

Alor settled himself on a chair in the veranda and said, attempting and failing to be nonchalant, "we are going to Australia."

Naynut stared at him, motionless and speechless. Alor allowed himself to smile. Nyanut broke into tears and hugged him. She kissed him on the forehead and the mouth. They were going to Ausralia after all.

Nyanut and little Achai joined the neighbours' celebrations while Alor set up the TV and switched to Al Jazeera. The headline read:

SOUTH SUDAN'S PRESIDENT
SAYS COUP ATTEMPT FOILED

The President started addressing the nation. Alor did not pay attention to much of what he was saying but to the men standing behind him.

There were generals and ministers he did not remember seeing during his time with the movement, guys he was sure were on the other side during the years of the struggle. Alor switched off the TV.

He did not want to watch more; he had seen enough. The cycle had begun again and even though he was going to Australia, he couldn't help but feel sad.

www.ingramcontent.com/pod-product-compliance
Lightning Source LLC
Chambersburg PA
CBHW010342170726
48283CB00009B/2928